REWRITE

Emmy Ellis

Chapter One

J anet watched George walk out of her office, thankful it wasn't out of her life. It had been touch and go for a while, their personal relationship ending the way it had, and she'd thought that was it, he'd avoid her forever like the stubborn bastard he was, but he'd actually come back. For therapy, nothing more, he'd made that abundantly clear, but she'd still get to see him often. Or as often as this latest need for her skills permitted. Who knew with him. He could ditch having help again. It wouldn't be the first time.

She didn't want that to happen. It *couldn't* happen. She'd made plans, and this go round, she intended to prove she could fix the past, that repeat mistakes *could* be mended. Yes, they'd split up, but she wanted him back. If she manipulated him the right way, he'd come running in the end. She knew for a fact she was the only woman he'd got that close to, the only one he'd allowed into a chink of his heart. Give it a few weeks, and she'd be back in his arms.

There was something he didn't know about her, though. A lot of things, actually, but the most recent was… She'd lied to him. She *had* been trying to change him, but not for the reasons he might think. Janet had wanted to fix him so he never had to go through what she did on the daily. Fighting with inner voices that pushed her to do things she didn't want to—or shouldn't want to. She wasn't on medication, but she ought to be. Instead, she'd done as much therapy on herself as she could to keep the little shits quiet.

In times of stress, though, they spoke the loudest, and recently, since she and George had parted ways, one of her personas had been piping up. Janet had submerged herself in helping Sienna, a woman who'd been desperate to get away from her controlling sister, Hannah. With Sienna to concentrate on, Janet had been able to douse the upset brought on by losing George as a lover. She'd had someone to fix, and for a while, it had worked. With no one to properly get her teeth into now, she'd found herself allowing one of the voices back in.

She had to maintain control over that.

She didn't have any more clients today, so she could go home and relax, although her mind was still jumping from the previous session with George. Sometimes, she missed running her practice on her own terms, taking on people *she* chose to. Nowadays she basically worked for the twins. All of their employees and residents were allowed 'free' counselling, but only if they really needed it, and The Brothers footed the bill. It made no odds to her, the money was the same whoever paid it, but she didn't feel like she owned her business fully anymore. All the NHS and private referrals had gone. The twins were her sole source of income—and they could make or break her.

She'd agreed to that, mainly to get in George's good graces, and the fact she didn't need to do that anymore in order to be his girlfriend grated on her. She'd given her word she'd be at their beck and call, and if she broke it now, just because they'd split up, she had no doubt George would teach her one of his lessons, no matter who she was. Who she'd once been to him.

She'd almost had him. In love with her. He'd fought it all the way; it had been fascinating to study him, watch him slowly come around to the idea that he could have a happy ever after. He'd lowered his defences and had cared. More than he'd thought he could. Or should. How annoying to have him in her grasp only for him to slip away. It reminded her of the mistake with Sean, and she gritted her teeth.

No, she would *not* have a repeat of that.

The Sean debacle, an experiment, hadn't gone to plan, and ever since, she'd tried, and failed, to obtain what she needed—someone to love her unconditionally, someone who'd never leave. With George, it had gone further than with any man with regards to having a 'normal' relationship, and she wasn't prepared to let it go and start again just yet.

One more push with him. One more stab at proving she was worthy.

She left her office and went into reception. Aster, her secretary, tended to the plants in the waiting area and turned to smile Janet's way.

"That's you done for the day, according to the diary," Aster said. "Unless you've got a walk-in clinic in mind?"

Janet preferred the in-depth, long-standing clients over solving problems quickly with the walk-ins. She enjoyed studying what she thought of as her subjects, placing them beneath the microscope, squashing them between two metaphorical glass slides until all of their secrets squished out, their cogs displaying how their minds worked, revealing their idiosyncrasies. Their reasons for struggling with mental health. She always hoped that one day she'd find that magic moment, the pivotal remedy, where she could fix them all—so she could fix herself. Selfish, the way she used her profession for her own ends, but so long as she played by the rules, what did her motivation matter? Once upon a time, she'd told anyone who'd asked that she'd gone into the field to be an angel and save people, the same as her friend, Billie, had with nursing. Such a lie. She filled her time with other people's problems so it minimised her own, kept the voices at bay. How wrong she'd been to believe she could control her illness that way. All it had done was highlight her issues so she compared herself to clients and found herself just as broken as them.

"Have you had any walk-in enquiries today, then?" Janet went behind the desk and flipped through the booking ledger, then checked it on the computer to ensure they matched, glad Aster was on the ball and everything was shipshape.

"Ichabod Ahearn could do with a chat." Aster wiped a weeping fig leaf with a damp cloth. "He phoned earlier in a bit of a state."

Janet perked up. Someone desperate usually equalled an interesting hour spent delving into their heads. Going home seemed less appealing now. "What sort of state?"

"He said Greg had told him to contact you because he's not been himself lately. When I asked what he needed help with, like you told me to whenever people want an appointment, Ichabod said he had an addiction."

"What kind?"

Aster rolled her eyes. "To cheese triangles."

"Um, what?"

"I know. Not the usual run-of-the-mill stuff."

"Right…" Janet glanced at her watch. "Okay, sod it, get him to come in for me now, please. He only lives down the road. He can have an hour, then we're going home; we should be out of here by three. It's about time me and you had an early day. Oh, and don't forget we're not opening tomorrow until two."

She had somewhere to be, somewhere no one around here knew she went. By rights, George and Greg should. *If* they'd had her followed prior to George first making contact with her for therapy, they'd have known. Then again, why would they suspect someone like her of being dodgy? Her disguise probably helped. Only people who'd known her years ago would recognise her with the short black wig and thick-rimmed glasses, no makeup in sight.

Aster spritzed the leaves of a fern with the mister then walked to the desk, Janet moving out of her way.

"How have you been?" Janet asked.

"A lot better, thanks. Talking to you helped a lot. It was the bit about other people's actions and perceptions of me not being my fault that made it click. Like, I can't control how they see me, and if they've got a problem with me being born male and choosing to live as a woman, that says a lot more about them than it does me."

Janet smiled. "Very true. Glad you're on the right track. If you need any more sessions, just shout."

"Thank you."

Aster phoned Ichabod. She'd been relatively easy to help compared to some because she *wanted* to have her mindset changed so she didn't blame herself for anything that had gone on in her life, things she hadn't had control over, and she'd learnt not to explain who she was inside; why should she? She was brilliant in this job and had settled into her new world well. That she was eyes and ears for the twins now was obvious, and it usually came with the territory after they'd helped someone out, people giving them Godlike status, but Janet wasn't hiding anything they needed to know about, so all was good.

She wandered into her office, staring at the blue throw cushion that still bore the imprint of

George's body—a body she'd once touched, craved, enjoyed. She should have been content to leave him broken—after all, it was what he wanted, to never be completely free of his dangerous persona, and he liked his jagged edges, his penchant for murder.

She did, too, although she'd never admit it to him.

He was who she longed to be, someone who could embrace every aspect of themselves and be comfortable with it, and her infatuation with him had started with a little seed, the roots of which were whispers in her mind: *If you can't be like him, live vicariously through him…*

She regularly spouted that she had a duty to inform the police if she knew beforehand what his plans were, but she'd never have seen it through, not with regards to him, nor his brother, seeing as they were so close and George loved Greg above all others. She'd claimed she wasn't, but she was jealous of that, what they shared, and many a time she'd entertained letting her dark side run free. Letting it kill Greg so George would turn to her for comfort and she'd be his axis instead.

She hadn't been able to bring herself to do it, though. It had gone wrong when she'd tried it with Sean, and doing it again would be too much like Charlene, the voice she tried so hard to ignore. The problem was, Charlene still lived inside her, went everywhere with her, lurking in her cells, her bones, her muscles, her mind. She may be in hiding most of the time, but it would only take one nod for the crazy cow to come out for good, that little thing called permission wreaking havoc.

The urge swept through her to get that mad, heady rush she used to feel, to become the user chasing the high from a fix. But no. She'd promised herself she'd be good after that mistake with Sean, and no matter how many times since then that she'd almost tipped over the edge, she'd held steady.

"Ichabod will be here in five," Aster called through.

"Thanks."

Janet made a coffee at the sideboard, then nipped to the toilet attached to her office. Washing her hands, she thought of how she'd approached the edge of the cliff during George's session, daring herself to step over, and if she had, he would never have known. She'd experienced the wicked, unethical, and utterly thrilling need to take him so far into his safe space that he was momentarily hypnotised. She called it The Place of Stillness. While she always preferred to guide people down a set of imaginary steps to that location where they felt calm and relaxed, usually a beach, it would only take a few more levels of that process to get them so deep she could make suggestions they wouldn't remember. She'd done it before, to someone she visited in prison every month, and they still didn't know what she'd done.

We all have crosses to bear.

As she walked out of the loo, she spied her coffee and made a beeline for it, drinking it too hot, needing the caffeine fix. She leaned her backside on the edge of her desk and stared out of the window, through the vertical blinds into the car park and beyond, waiting for her client to arrive.

A couple of minutes later, forty-year-old Ichabod appeared and seemed to walk like a daddy longlegs, his somewhat airy steps giving the impression he was made of nothing substantial. His thin body, encased in a baggy black T-shirt and white skinny jeans, sprouted up from trainers that looked too big. Size elevens on a slim-build body, and he reminded her of a clown.

She finished her coffee and went to make him one. If she remembered rightly, he liked a latte with two Sweetex. The machine poured, and she tried to wrap her head around how she'd deal with his cheese triangle addiction. The same as any other? She supposed so.

A throat cleared, and she turned. Ichabod hovered in the office doorway, his long, wispy brown hair hanging limp.

"Come in, come in," she said, gesturing to the Irishman, playing the part of the good little therapist George expected her to be. She closed the door. "How have you been?"

Ichabod sat on the comfortable armchair, making his own imprint in the blue cushion, erasing George completely. "Strugglin' tae feck."

"With the cheese triangles?" Janet sat opposite on the sofa and placed his coffee on the low table between them.

Ichabod shook his head, frowning. He bit a nail. Spat it out. "That was just somethin' I said so Aster didn't get nosy."

"Nosy?"

"Ye know, tell the twins stuff." His eyes became hooded, as if something awful loitered in his mind. "I can't be doing wid that eejit droppin' me in it about a job. No offence, Aster's a good girl, but ye know how it is."

"So you want to discuss a job you've done for them?"

"Yeah, but I don't want them knowin' I've been gossipin'."

"Right, well, you know I won't say anything." That was a lie, she would if it had the potential to destroy the twins—if she wanted George in her bed again, she had to have his back. "Client confidentiality an' all that."

"Yeah, ye said that before. I was checkin', that's all. Too many people say shit and don't mean it."

"Don't they just." She hadn't meant to say that out loud, and she'd been referring to herself; she said so much she didn't mean, but it was too late now. "So what's troubling you, then?"

"There was this girl. Kallie."

"Right…"

"Her out there, Aster," he jerked his thumb at the closed door, "a while back she told The

Brothers that Kallie was going tae be a problem. She was, there's no question of that, I just didn't like havin' tae, umm, help kill her. The twins were too busy tae do it, see, all that stuff wid the refugees."

"Why was she a problem?" Janet already knew, but this was the sort of question she was expected to ask.

"Put it this way, Kallie would have got them in the shit if she opened her mouth about her mate who'd been involved with all of Aster's bollocks. Ye know, when her dad went weird."

Janet remembered it well. She'd walked Aster though the fallout emotions afterwards. "What sort of shit do you mean?"

"Well, Sarah had gone tae Italy, if ye catch me drift, except she hadn't, had she, she was dead. This Kallie, she was goin' tae get hold of the pigs in Italy and ask questions. Like, she was sayin' Sarah wouldn't have just gone off the way she did, so somethin' must have happened tae her. Kallie was goin' tae cause ructions."

"So you had to shut her up."

"Yeah, except it doesn't sit well, because she was me feckin' goddaughter."

"Oh."

"Yeah, but I did it anyway, because that's what ye sign up for wid them twins, but it doesn't mean I have tae like it, does it. So I'm struggling wid that."

"Okay, let's break this down so it isn't such a jumble in your head. You agreed to work for the twins and do what they say."

"Yeah."

"If you don't do it, you'll be in trouble with them."

"Yeah. And the rest."

"So in order to save yourself, you have to do things to others." *Am I saying this to myself or him?*

"Yeah, and I don't mind normally. Like, I *enjoy* it. But this one, she was me mate's kid, known her fer years. They're broken, the family, and it's my fault."

"If it wasn't you, it would have been someone else."

"I know that, but wid all the others, I haven't had tae see the family getting upset. I put them out of me mind, don't think twice. But Kallie…"

"Did you tell the twins about your relationship with her?"

"No."

"They would have given the job to someone else if you had. They'd have understood."

"I know, and that's what's gettin' tae me. I didn't want tae show weakness, so I did it. I'm the nastiest kind of bastard. Even went tae her funeral, so I did. It was my choice tae proceed, even though I had options, so there's only one person I can blame here, and that's me. How do I stop feeling so bad?"

"By talking it through until it doesn't feel so draining. I have another walk-in tomorrow afternoon if you want me to put your name down." One bonus about catering to people on The Cardigan Estate meant they opened up to her about things she hadn't previously known. Ichabod might just prove to be a great source of information she could use later. With what, she didn't know, but she liked to hedge her bets.

"All right." He drank his coffee, thinking, staring into space for a while.

Janet let him. She got paid whether he spoke or not.

"Ye'll tell the twins I like a bit tae much Dairylea if they ask why I came, then, yeah? Or The Laughing Cow."

"Even if they ask, I won't tell them your business. They won't even know about the cheese."

"Good. Just checkin'."

"You check a lot."

"It's a part of me makeup."

He spent the rest of the session detailing how he'd helped to kill Kallie then going to The Angel for a pint as if it hadn't happened. Acting shocked when his friend had told him the bad news.

"Feckin' terrible," he said. "I'm a terrible, terrible man, so I am. The worst."

Chapter Two

*J*anet trembled. She stared at the dead mouse — the squashed, dead mouse — and didn't understand what had happened. Blood stained the back garden path, and a blob of…something poked out of a split in the furry body. Why was the mouse like that? It had been running around just now. She'd thought of catching it, squeezing it really hard in her ten-year-old-girl hands, but there was no way she'd have actually done it. These urges she had, they were wrong, she knew that, but she still had them, and it didn't help that she was encouraged to act them out.

"What the hell is wrong with you?" Mum hissed, hands on hips, her brown hair spilling from the high bun at the top of her head, as if she'd grabbed at it like she always did when she got angry.

Janet looked away from the woman who told her regularly that if she wasn't careful, people would tell the social about her behaviour. The words 'the social' scared Janet every time. It meant being taken away from Mum, being put in a house with other naughty kids, or worse, in a big place where there were dormitories and no cuddles.

"I didn't do that," Janet said, fear bringing on more shakes.

She'd missed a patch of time again and tried to bring it back to mind, but it remained hidden. Mum thought she was lying when she said she didn't do the bad things, but she wasn't. It was the truth. Why wouldn't she believe her? Why would Janet even lie about something like that?

"Don't even think of lying to me, my girl. I watched you through the kitchen window. You stamped on it."

Janet couldn't remember doing it, but if Mum said she had, she must have.

"It wasn't doing any harm," Mum went on, "so why did you kill it?"

"It…it was Maggie."

"Oh, don't start that again. What have I told you about making up stories, making up people to blame? Where is this Maggie, eh? Why didn't I see her stamp on the mouse? Why is it, when you say it's her, she's never *here*?"

Maggie and Charlene had lived loudly inside Janet's head ever since Dad had walked out last year. He'd gone, hadn't even told her he was leaving. Janet had got up the next day and he hadn't been there, but his stuff was. That disappeared one day later on, while she'd been at school. Mum had been a right mess for weeks after. Janet hadn't done any better, crying for him every night. She still did. There was no more Monopoly on a Sunday night after tea, him always winning, and Janet hadn't played chequers in ages. He was a lovely man, although he had said to Mum the night before he'd gone that he couldn't cope with Janet anymore, whatever that meant. That was the only part she could recall.

It was confusing. Janet had been good, she hadn't done any of the naughty stuff when he'd been here, so why couldn't he cope with her? Was she naughty and didn't know it, like what had happened with the *mouse? Why hadn't they told her off, though? Why couldn't she remember if they had? And what was so bad that it meant he had to leave?*

Her two 'friends' had helped her when she'd been lonely, when she'd cried, when she'd felt like she wanted to run and run, to where, she didn't know. Maggie was the worst one, she told Janet to do bad things, and doing them helped, too, because it took away some of the horrible feelings inside her. For a while after obeying Maggie, Janet was happier. Charlene wasn't as pushy. She suggested things to do but didn't take over her as quickly as Maggie did.

Janet had told Mum about them, and that was why she thought Janet was seeing people who weren't there. She worried people would think Janet was a nutter. That wasn't a nice name. The other nutter around here, old Mr Nasonova, people took the piss out of him, crossed the road if he was around, and talked about him behind his back, saying he was off his rocker.

Did they talk about her like that?

No. Mum said she'd hide Janet being weird, that Dad wouldn't be telling anyone either because he was ashamed. They didn't want people pointing the finger.

Mum glanced over the chicken-wire fence to the next-door neighbour's kitchen window. "You'd better hope Irene didn't see you doing that." She checked her watch. "Ah, you're safe. She'll be down Kwik Save by now. Good job, too, else she'd ring the social. She already thinks I can't cope without your dad around. Any excuse, and she'll be on the blower." Another stare at the mouse. "You can pick it up, I'm not touching it. I'll get some newspaper."

Mum steamed off to the house and disappeared inside. Maggie wanted to know what it would feel like if Mum walked out like Dad had, but Charlene told her to shut up. Janet told them both to be quiet and looked at the mouse again.

"You shouldn't have done that, Maggie," she whispered. "I'm in trouble now."

Her friends had gone, leaving her to deal with this by herself, and she wished she could go back to how it was before, when Dad was here and Maggie and Charlene weren't. Or they were, and Janet just didn't know it. If he came back, they'd go away for good, wouldn't they?

Mum reappeared with a newspaper and thrust it into Janet's hands. "Use the spade to scoop it up, and when you've wrapped it, put it in the dustbin out the front. After that, you can come and get the bucket and brush and scrub that path. Then we'll be having words."

Janet's tummy rolled over. She didn't like having words. There had been a lot of those this past year, where they sat at the kitchen table and Mum tried to 'get to the bottom' of what was going on. Where she pleaded for Janet to just be a good girl and not be so strange.

She forced back stinging tears and, once Mum had gone inside, Janet got on with clearing up the mess. It was horrible, she needed Maggie or Charlene to come and help her, but the sense of being completely alone, one she'd learnt to recognise, meant she'd have to face this by herself. When they weren't inside her, it was like she wasn't all there, parts of her were missing.

Sometimes, it was nice having her friends in her head. But days like today, she wished they'd never come. Mum didn't believe they even existed, they were a figment of Janet's imagination, and if Janet told the girls at school, they'd laugh and call her Mr Nasonova and stop playing with her. Maybe Billie wouldn't, she was the nicest, but Janet couldn't risk having no mates. There was this boy, he didn't have any, and he sat on the wall around the playground, watching but never joining in, because when he'd tried it, everyone had told him to sod off.

No one wanted to be like Davey Bartram.

Janet dragged her heels walking down the side of the house and out the front. She lifted the bin lid and put the newspaper package inside, then leaned on the gate beside the sprawling bush and watched the kids playing in the street. If she'd come out here earlier, the mouse would still be alive, but she hadn't, and it was dead, and it was all Maggie's fault.

The Sackville lads played football, three brothers who all looked the same, except they were different heights. Their sister played French skipping with two other girls who lived down the end, and Irene's rabble, as Mum called them, took turns with the hopscotch they'd chalked onto the pavement. Janet didn't want to hang around with any of them, that's why she'd stayed in the garden and waited for Billie to get back from town with her mum.

"Want to play with us?" one of Irene's lot asked, a girl with straggly, mud-coloured hair and a filthy face.

Mum said Irene was a dirty cow, she didn't do much housework and smoked her days away at the kitchen table—apparently her yellowing nets proved that—and Janet was to keep away from all of them, especially because she was so weird these days.

"No ta," Janet said and smiled, because smiling meant they wouldn't be mean to her, and not being mean meant Irene wouldn't ring the social to get back *at Mum out of spite. They'd had a big falling-out, see, about the crow Maggie had killed, and Irene liked to cause trouble. "I've got to wash the garden path for me mum."*

She skipped off down the side of the house. The bucket, bubbles foaming over the top, had already been left on the path, and a brush lay beside it. Janet got on her knees and scrubbed the blood away, then cleaned the spade, flicking off a glob of red goo. She poured the remaining water onto the grass and went inside, leaving the bucket and brush on the kitchen floor by the sink unit.

She washed her hands.

Mum sat at the table and poked a finger on it several times. "Close the back door and sit."

Janet did as she was told. The seat, hard under her bum, brought back memories of all the times she'd sat here playing board games when there'd been the three of them.

"Listen to me," Mum said. "You keep talking about this Maggie and Charlene as if they're real people, and it's got to stop. I know kids have imaginary friends, and that's okay up to a point, but you're too old for that business. What isn't okay is to stamp on a mouse and all the other things you've done, then blame it on them. You have to admit it's you, understand? Lying about

it isn't right. Pretending you didn't do it and can't remember is wrong."

"But it is them. It's like they're real people inside me. Voices. They talk and everything."

Mum frowned. "What do you mean, voices? You don't see them as people, like you'd see Billie?"

"No, they're in me."

Mum reared back, her face paling. "Dear God. Um… Let me just think for a minute." She drummed her short nails on the wicker coaster beside the jar of dandelions Janet had picked for her yesterday. "You say they're in you. What do you mean?"

"They talk in my head, tell me to do stuff."

"Shit." Mum hardly ever swore, so this must be bad. "Okay, right, you don't tell anyone about this, understand? No one. We have to keep it a secret."

"But keeping secrets is naughty, and you just said lying about it isn't right."

"I know I did, but sometimes things change." Mum stared outside through the glass in the back door. "I should take you to the doctor," she muttered. Then, "No, we'll deal with this together." She looked at Janet. "What sort of things do they tell you to do?"

"All what you've said I've done, plus Charlene's always trying to get me to have fights at school and stuff, like when someone gets on my nerves, she tells me to punch them. I can make her go away if I want, but Maggie, she's too strong. She does things, like she tells me what to do, I say no, then the next thing, it's already done and I don't know when it happened."

"Like with the mouse?"

Janet nodded, her bottom lip wobbling. "I don't like it, I want them to leave me alone, but they won't."

Mum got up and crouched, gathering a crying Janet in her arms. "We'll sort this out, all right? But listen to me." She pulled back and cupped Janet's face. "You really mustn't tell anyone, especially not Dad if you see him. You know Mr Nasonova, yes? Do you know where he goes when he isn't around for a while?"

Janet shook her head.

"He has to go to a special place sometimes, when he gets too bad. They keep him there to make him better with tablets. I don't want you to go there. If I do what your dad wants and tell the doctor about what you said, they might make you go somewhere like that, and I couldn't stand to be without you."

Janet's heart lurched, and she sobbed, fear giving her the shakes. Mum hugged her again, stroked her hair, and whispered that everything would be okay. They'd get rid of Maggie and Charlene, then everything could go back to normal.

"But it won't be normal, not until Dad comes home."

Mum eased back again. "What's he got to do with this?"

"Maggie and Charlene didn't get inside me until he left."

Mums mouth thinned. "No, love, you said they were there long before that."

"I didn't."

"You did."

"I only remember them coming when Dad went."

Mum spoke as if to herself. "He must have triggered something. That bastard's got a lot to answer for." She shook her head. "Go and play out the front while I nip to the Sickle and have it out with him."

Mum had said bastard, so it was really, **really** bad.

"Go on, love, off you go."

Janet wiped her eyes and, the remnants of sobs still hiccupping, went out and stood at the front gate. Everything seemed better once she spotted Billie clambering out of the car three doors down. Janet waved, and Billie called to her mum that she was playing out, then ran to Janet.

"I've got new marbles," Billie said and held them up. She frowned. "Have you been crying?"

Janet couldn't tell the truth about why. "A bit. I miss me dad."

Billie shrugged. "He's a pig, my mum said, so don't waste time missing him."

Janet opened the gate and crouched on the path with Billie. Dad was lovely, wasn't he? "Why's he a pig?"

"He gets up to stuff. That's all I know."

"Up to stuff?"

"Yeah." Billie shared the marbles out.

Mum thundered past, on her way to the pub, her handbag slapping her leg.

"What's up with her?" Billie whispered.

"She's going to have words with me dad."

"My mum has those with mine, and they shout a lot."

That's what Janet was worried about. Shouting would mean he wouldn't come home. Dad wasn't a shouter, he was quiet, but Mum, she was loud sometimes.

She remembered what Mum had said to Billie's only last week: "It's the quiet ones you need to worry about, obviously."

What did that mean?

Chapter Three

Ichabod sat in Debbie's kitchen in her flat above The Angel. She fussed around with a pod machine, making coffee, not in the least bit interested as to why George and Greg had asked to meet him there, nor why her flat was the chosen place to chat. Ichabod supposed she was used to helping them out, and they trusted her. Debbie was like family to them.

They didn't have a base like Ron Cardigan had. Sensible, as it meant none of their enemies had a place they could watch, then spring out on the twins and do them some damage. The Brothers had learnt from Ron's reign, they'd watched his fuck-ups and successes and acted accordingly. Ichabod had met them in various random locations since he'd started working for them. A lot of the business talks he was needed for were done in their BMW, Greg driving around while George issued orders.

Ichabod had got lucky, accidentally on purpose stumbling into the twins' path not long after Ron had died—he'd needed a steady income, and as they'd known him anyway, they'd taken him on. Ichabod had been used by Ron as a runner, basically, not really doing much other than taking messages or keeping watch here and there. George had said he'd heard Ichabod needed some cash, a job, and he'd been taken on as a watcher in the alley at first, keeping an eye on the girls who worked Debbie's corner when the usual men weren't available or needed a holiday.

It hadn't been a permanent position, though. He'd get a call, he'd turn up for however many hours, then wait until the next time he was needed.

Thankfully, George had taken note of Ichabod's punctuality, his ability to do his job without griping, and he'd finally got his permanent place in their ranks—someone sent to get information out of people, without them knowing he was doing it. He was a bit like Sonny Bates in that respect, a bloke no one took much notice of, and because of his friendly Irish countenance, they trusted him with their secrets if he bought them a few bevvies.

Many a time, Ichabod's information had given The Brothers the green light to wade in and sort out those who weren't following Cardigan rules. Seeing Janet, being one of the only people to even know they were watching her, was a privilege and a step up the ladder. He'd prove to the two big men he could be trusted even more—no way would he tell anyone else what he was doing.

Ichabod had come from Ireland as a child with his mammy and daddy, at first settling in Liverpool, then Daddy's job had brought them to London. His parents were dead now, God rest their weary souls, and to be in with George and Greg had replaced the family feel that had been

33

missing since their passing. And he wanted a coveted place at their table like Debbie had. He'd do whatever it took to get it. Obey, scheme for them, hurt people.

He craved acceptance.

The kettle boiled, cutting off with a rowdy click, steam hitting the side of a wall cupboard, condensation drizzling. Debbie stripped the lid off a Pot Noodle, rummaged in the drawer for a fork, and slapped it on the worktop.

"You can put your own water in," she said to George. "You whinged last time, saying I filled it too high."

"There's an art to it," George said. "Just enough sauce for a few dips of bread, and it can't be pissy."

Debbie absently handed Ichabod a coffee, on autopilot. "Like I said, do it your-bloody-self." She put a pod in the machine for George—Greg already had his cuppa—then walked to the door. "Lock up after yourself. Take the spare keys with you in case you need to come back—I won't be here. I'm off to Moon's for a couple of nights. We've got some quality time on the cards. He's just come out the other side of that big bust and needs a bit of a rest. If I don't force him to park his arse, he'll just keep going. Too much work and no play makes Moon a dull boy."

Ichabod didn't know what the big bust was, but the twins seemed to. They nodded, and while it would be nice to be told, he respected the fact they didn't discuss the intricacies of Moon's business in front of him. It meant they'd afford him the same courtesy, keeping his shenanigans to themselves, too. And if he didn't ask what had gone on, they wouldn't think he was a plant, someone sent by another leader to spy on them.

He eyed Debbie, wishing things had been different, that he'd had a set of balls and approached her way back when. It was too late, though. Most people knew about her being with Moon now. Ichabod had fancied her from the moment he'd clapped eyes on her, although he wasn't daft enough to think she'd be interested in someone like him, hence him having no balls. Not after she'd been with Ron Cardigan, then, after he'd died, swearing off men. Moon was a lucky bastard and must be special if she'd agreed to be his bit of stuff.

Ichabod had one of those moments where he contemplated what-if. What if he'd told her he liked her? What if she'd said they could go on a date? Where would they be now if that had happened?

Pointless tormenting yourself, ye eejit. She's in love wid someone else.

Debbie closed the kitchen door, and Greg, sitting beside Ichabod at the breakfast bar, drank some coffee. George stabbed at the noodles to break them up, then left them to soak. A plate of buttered tiger bread sat nearby. The sight of food had Ichabod's stomach rumbling. He'd get an early dinner in the pub downstairs after this little get-together.

No one spoke until the slam of the front door let them know they were alone.

George leaned his arse against the worktop. "So, what did you make of her today?"

Ichabod didn't have to ask who George meant. "She behaved like any other therapist again. She's going tae be a hard nut tae crack, so tae speak. She's confident, shows no sign of vulnerability. I can't see how I can get into her psyche. She's tae clever tae let anyone in. Someone like me anyway."

"Everyone's got a weak spot. I still don't know why she lied to me." George gave the noodles a bit of a poke with the fork. "We did the research on her yonks ago before I chose her as a therapist, and nothing came up about her omission."

Greg snorted. "Until it did."

Ichabod had heard all this before when they'd recruited him to spy on Janet. George must be talking more to himself, speaking his thoughts to get his head straight. Ichabod had been sent to Janet to see if he could get her to open up to him. He'd only been a couple of times so far so hadn't got a proper bead on her yet, and maybe he never would.

He'd lied to her about Kallie. Someone else had bumped her off, and she certainly wasn't his feckin' goddaughter. He'd congratulated himself on thinking up that little story, and if he wasn't mistaken, Janet had been intrigued. Maybe she'd already known about the hassle Aster had been through but hadn't found out where Kallie had gone. Ichabod couldn't imagine George telling her all the ins and outs of the firm. He'd be a wally if he did that. Not that Ichabod would have the guts to say that to his face. George was a mad bastard and then some.

"That's Janine for you," Greg said. "Doing a bloody good job."

Their copper. Ichabod had never met her but had heard she was good. Better than their previous DI, that prick, Rod Clarke.

George clenched his jaw. "I fucking well asked Clarke to run a check on Janet, and he said she was clean, hence why I went ahead with the therapy. If I'd known what I know now, I'd never have got involved with her."

Ah, so Clarke buggered up?

Greg chuffed out air. "We all know who Clarke really was now. I bet he found it amusing not telling you Janet was at a party when a kid got murdered. By her best fucking friend."

"Tosser."

Ichabod, surprised by that revelation, controlled his expression. The reason the twins were after Janet hadn't been mentioned until now. He sipped some coffee, wondering where this was going. If they wanted just an update on Janet's behaviour earlier at her office, there wasn't much he could pass on. She certainly wouldn't discuss a murder with the likes of him, would she? He sifted through the conversation for any snippet that might point to her being a wrong un.

"I've racked me brains," he said, "and the only thing I can think of that was a bit off was this. I told her tae tell you two, if ye asked, that I've got an addiction tae cheese triangles, right—"

"What?" Greg choked out.

Ichabod blushed at his off-the-cuff excuse for needing therapy. It had popped into his mind on the phone to Aster, and he'd run with it. "It was so she thought I trusted her wid me shit, like we're in cahoots, me and Janet. With her knowin' I'd lied tae Aster about why I needed an appointment, she might trust me more. She said, 'Even if they ask, I won't tell them your business.' That's all well and good, isn't it, it's what ye'd expected someone like her tae say. So I said, 'Good. Just checkin'.' Now I said that tae see if she was loyal tae ye and got on the blower tae let ye know I'm shifty and mebbe someone tae watch out for. And she said, 'You check a lot.' That could just be a general observation, like she's clocked I'm wary of who I speak tae and what I say, or it could be her filing that away, warnin' herself tae be careful what she says tae me." He paused. "I'm clutchin' at straws, aren't I."

"Could be something or it could be nothing." George dipped folded bread into his noodle sauce and bit off a big chunk. Chewed. "I'll keep it up here, though." He tapped his temple.

"Like we agreed, I'm seein' her again tomorrow afternoon," Ichabod said. "What bullshit are ye wantin' me tae feed her this time?"

George smiled, another piece of bread held aloft. "Tell her you've got to kill someone. A similar situation to what Janine dug up for us about her. You're after a bloke who killed a kid in their own home."

Ichabod nodded. "But it's not like she's goin' tae pipe up and tell me about what happened tae her friend now, is it?"

"No, but you can gauge her reaction," Greg said. "See if she flinches. We might get lucky and she offers you some sage advice."

There was something bothering Ichabod. "I don't want tae speak out of turn, but if her friend's the killer, why do ye need me tae get Janet talkin' about it?"

George had finished all the bread and dug the fork into the noodles, twirling it around. "Because it's the sort of shit you'd tell someone you're getting close to, isn't it?"

"I doubt I can get close tae her, not like that."

George glanced at Greg who nodded.

"What I'm about to tell you stays in this room," George said.

Ichabod bristled. "Of course it feckin' well does. What do ye take me for?"

"Sorry, but only a select few know about this, unless she's blabbed to someone and I'm not aware of it." George took a deep breath. "I was seeing her."

Ichabod didn't get why they were going over old ground. "I know, for the therapy."

"No, *seeing* her, seeing her."

"Aww, feck." Ichabod marvelled at how the twins could go about, doing shit, and no one knew. He thought he had his finger on the pulse of Cardigan, but he hadn't seen that one coming.

"I got blindsided and thought we were going somewhere," George said. "Then she fucked it up by trying to mess with my mind, wanting to control me, to label me. But we were far enough down the road that she should have told me about such a big thing in her past, yet she didn't. Why? If she's got nothing to hide, why keep it to herself?"

Greg sniffed. "It wasn't like *you* fully opened up to *her*, bruv."

George stared at him as if he wanted to punch his lights out. "I know, you pleb, but women are a bit more open like that. Aren't they?" He looked at Ichabod for the answer, maybe because the twins weren't au fait with relationships.

Ichabod bobbed his head. "In my experience, yes. And I get what ye mean. If she was talkin' weddin' bells, she should have told ye any dark secrets by that point. Although that depends on how long ye were together. I'm not prying, I don't need tae know, I was just stating a fact. Some people take years tae properly open up."

"I get that, but just say I married her, then ten years down the line, she springs that on me. Fuck's sake. I like all cards out on the table, everyone knows that. *She* should know that." George got on with eating his noodles.

Greg drummed his fingertips on the breakfast bar. "Fucking bitch. I *knew* there was something off about her. And there was you, thinking I was just jealous because you fucked off out with her of an evening."

"You were, though," George said through a mouthful of food.

"Shut your face. It was more than that. She's got this entitled air about her, the bossy cow, and that got my goat, but there's something else."

"Like what?" Ichabod asked. "She was more involved in the murder than the police think?"

George nodded. "That could be it. They're best friends. One kills a kid. What if Janet saw it but lied under oath, saying she didn't? Not a good look when she's a therapist. Could she get struck off for that? Or what if she had a hand in it? Janine said the killer, a woman called Billie Haiden, was heavily under the influence of alcohol and LSD and can't remember killing. What if she also can't remember *Janet* being there?"

"Sounds a bit pie in the sky," Greg said. "Surely Janine would have told us if Janet was a suspect. It would have been in the files."

"Janine didn't get a chance to read them thoroughly," George said.

"Maybe Janet didn't want tae talk about it because it's painful," Ichabod suggested. "We've all seen shit we'd rather not chat about."

"True." Greg finished his coffee. "Right, you go and see her tomorrow, as planned, for a walk-in session. Give her all the old guff about you having to sort a bloke who killed a kid. Make out

43

you don't want to do the job or something. If she phones George about you being hesitant, we know she's on the level—with regards to informing us of things anyway. In the meantime, follow her. I *know* she's hiding something, I've sensed it all along, and I want to root out what it is."

"Get yourself a bit of grub first, Ich." George fished in his pocket and brought an envelope out. He tossed it on the breakfast bar. "That should see you right for a few days."

Ichabod opened it. A wedge of fifty-pound notes. He really *had* gone up in their estimation. Proud of himself for proving he was worth trusting, he stuck his chest out. "Ye're a good man, so ye are." He popped it in his jacket pocket, thinking of the bills he could pay off with that amount of money. He stood. "I'll pass on where she goes and who she sees, that goes without saying."

"I'll get Dwayne to let you know what car to use and where to pick it up." George smiled. "Don't look so uneasy, the plates will be changed, just don't speed and bring attention to yourself else you'll be had up for nicking the car. If that happens and you're banged up in a holding cell, it'll fuck up our mission with Janet. We can't send Will or Martin to her in your place because she knows they wouldn't cross us, whereas you, she has no idea what you're like." He waved at Ichabod's appearance. "You might want to get changed an' all. Wear something she wouldn't expect you to put on, so she doesn't recognise you, and sort that fucking hair. Put it in a man bun or summat."

"Don't ye worry. I've got a suit, cap, and glasses. She won't suspect anythin' is up. Message me her address. I'll keep an eye on her place this evenin'."

"If she doesn't go out once it hits midnight, go home," Greg said. "Then go back for six in the morning."

"Will do."

George put his pot in the bin. "She rarely goes out at night anyway, so you should have an easy time of it."

Ichabod nodded at them in turn and left the flat, his footsteps loud on the steel steps running down the side of the building. He walked along the driveway and turned left onto the pavement, nipping into the packed pub. At the bar, he asked Lisa, the manager, for pie and mash with liquor, plus a Diet Coke as he was driving, then he sat in a corner to wait for his food.

His phone pinged twice. Janet's home address and the location of a car stolen by Dwayne, the fella who dealt with whatever vehicles the twins needed. It was a silver Saab, the reg number giving the impression it was a vanity plate, and the keys had been left on the front-right tyre a couple of streets away outside The Baker's Dough pub. The hot, sticky summer had almost come to an end, autumn would be knocking soon, so a quick walk round there would be nice, seeing as the sun was hanging around. He'd nip home after and get changed.

He ate his meal and thought about George's confession. Him and Janet? She didn't seem the type of woman who'd do well with a gangster for a husband. She was too headstrong, wouldn't take kindly to doing as she was told, but maybe he'd got that wrong. Some women who had high-powered jobs liked having a bloke who called the shots. Yes, she clearly kept shit the twins did to herself, but to actually be emotionally involved with one of them? She had to be off her nut if she thought she could tame George. As for messing with his mind, labelling him. What had George meant by that?

What the hell had she been playing at by trying to control him? *No one* could, and she should know that.

Ichabod aimed to find out what she was up to. He wanted more envelopes stuffed with money. George had given him at least two grand just now, a tidy sum. It seemed Ichabod had *really* moved up the ranks if they were trusting him with something like this.

About feckin' time. I've been as loyal as they come.

Chapter Four

Janet stood outside The Sheaf and Sickle, peering through a square pane of the bay window. It had been months since Maggie had killed the mouse, and she stamped her feet, her baggy wellies failing to keep out the chill. Janet had been told by Mum to stay away from here, from Dad, but Charlene reckoned it was a good idea to find out why he'd said he couldn't cope with Janet. Maggie just wanted to poke him in the eye

49

with a lit cigarette, but that was well naughty, and Janet had said no. Anyway, where would they even get a fag from to be able to do that?

"You could nick one from Irene."

"No."

The wind rushed up the street, bringing crisp wrappers, an empty beer can, and a strip of plastic with it, the kind used on packing boxes. It whipped her shin on the way past, then tossed and spiralled in the air.

Janet hunched her shoulders and turned her attention back to the pub. Dad sat at the bar with a blonde woman, and she held a small baby in a blue shawl, other people cooing over it.

Janet shouldn't go inside, Mum would tell her off if she found out, but Dad was there, he hadn't been the last few times Janet had checked, and she might not get the chance to speak to him again for ages.

It was Sunday, and the place was done up with blue bunting, balloons, and a sign above a long table covered with food read HAPPY CHRISTENING DAY! So the woman was a God-botherer if she'd christened the kid, that's what Mum would call her, someone who believed in something that wasn't even there, something you couldn't see, some bloke who lived in Heaven or whatever.

Was Janet a God-botherer then, because she couldn't see Maggie and Charlene?

Dad kissed the baby's head, which was weird. You didn't go round doing that, did you, not unless it was your child. He took it and held it against his chest, rubbing his nose on the top of its head.

"Do you reckon he loves it?" *Charlene asked.*

"It looks like him," *Maggie said.*

Janet didn't like the sound of that. "Shut up."

It did look like him, though. Was it his? Had he left Janet and Mum for that woman and she'd had a baby? The divorce had come through not long after the mouse incident, Mum crying because that was the final nail in the coffin of her marriage — she'd muttered that while ferreting in the cupboard for a glass to go with her gin. How could Dad have another kid when he didn't care for the one he already had? Was that why Mum had told her not to come here? Because she'd have seen the woman and Dad kissing or something?

"You should go inside and ask him what's going on," *Charlene said.*

Maggie huffed. "And smack the baby on the head with one of those ashtrays."

"I can't do that!"

Smoke hung thick in the air around the bar, and Janet vaguely recalled Mum saying smoking around

51

babies was bad, yet all those people inside, they were doing it. Muted laughter came from a table to the left, and Janet recognised Dad's workmates, Pete and Norman. They used to buy her an ice cream from the van on the Fridays when she and Mum went to meet Dad from the building site that time he did carpentry work on those new houses.

Why couldn't things be like they used to, where everything seemed happier? When Mum laughed a lot and baked cakes on a Sunday for tea after she'd done the ironing, Dad coming home from the Sickle and twirling her round, her saying he was full of beer and needed a nap to sleep it off. Later, they'd play board games, and then it was bath time and bed.

Janet wiped a tear away, another gust of wind jostling her, trying to sneak under the hem of her woolly hat.

"Don't cry over him," Maggie said. "Billie's already told you he's a waste of space, and now we can see why."

Janet blinked and, in her head, asked Maggie to leave her alone. She was so pushy and spiteful, and as Mum had let Janet know what she'd been getting up to before Dad had left, it was Maggie who they needed to get rid of. The list of naughty things she'd done shocked Janet, who'd apparently been smacked and shouted at by Dad for it, but she didn't remember. *Maybe she didn't want to, because admitting Dad had smacked her meant he wasn't as lovely as she thought. It was as if sections of her life had been rubbed out, and no matter how hard she tried to imagine herself doing those things, receiving the punishments, it was blank.*

Kicking a cat in the street.

Shooting a crow with one of the Sackville brothers' air guns.

Stamping on a dog's tail while it waited for its owner outside the shops.

Stabbing Dad's hand with a fork at dinner.

There was more, but Janet couldn't stand to think about it. Such horrible things, so no wonder Dad had buggered off. It was her fault he'd gone.

No, it was Maggie's.

"I only do what you're thinking," *Maggie said.*

"I don't want you to do anything ever again." Janet wished there was a magic pill she could take that would send Maggie and Charlene away and bring Dad back, but if that was his baby, it would mean having it in the house. Mum wouldn't like that.

Dad glanced over and caught sight of her. He stared, his mouth opening a bit, then handed the baby back to the woman and said something in her ear. The lady turned and peered through the window, clutching

53

the baby tighter, and she went and sat with someone who looked like her, a sister maybe. Dad walked towards the door, and Janet's stomach muscles bunched up. What would she say to him? What would he say to her?

He came out, putting his coat on, and took her elbow, then snatched it away as though he couldn't stand to touch her. He led her down the road to Mr Balakrishnan's little shop, all the while glancing across the street at the houses, like he didn't want anyone to see him with her, then he unlatched the gate, ushering her into the yard. She opened her mouth to ask him...what, she didn't know, and snapped it shut again.

"What do you want?" He stood back, far away from her.

She shrugged. "I wanted to see you."

"You can't be anywhere near me, Janet. I don't trust you."

"What?"

"The things you've done, the way you are..." He showed her the raised line of four scars on the back of his hand from the fork stab.

"But..."

"You're...you're weird, all right? I can't handle it."

"I didn't know I did that stuff."

"I don't want to hear all that rubbish again. You did it, we saw you, or other people did, and it's not on. Lying about being cruel. Being nasty to animals. Jesus, I can't even look at you." He turned to study the back of the shop.

"Maggie did it, she did everything."

"So you said when you got caught, but there is no Maggie, you made her up."

Janet frowned. Maggie must have been there before Dad left, like Mum said. Why hadn't Janet known? "How come you don't come to see me? Sara at school, her dad doesn't live with them, but she sees him every Saturday. They go to the zoo and stuff."

"I can't see you."

"Why not?"

"I don't want to see you. Just go home, will you? Bugger off." He walked to the gate and opened it. He did that thing Janet did when she listened to Maggie and Charlene, cocking his head, but there was no way he had voices inside him, was there? Maybe he was just thinking. "I don't want you. I don't love you anymore."

Then he was gone, leaving Janet with burning eyes and a growing lump in her throat.

"Go after him," *Maggie said.* "Push him into the road and get him run over. Make him die."

Janet legged it from the yard and chased her father up the street, tears blurring her vision. She rammed into him, shouting, "I hate you! I bloody hate you!"

He spun round and gripped her wrist, pinching the skin where his thumb and fingertip met. "Listen to me, you fucking little weirdo. Fuck. Off. Got it?" *He let her go and jogged to the Sickle, pushing the door open and vanishing inside.*

Janet stood there, hate filling her, Charlene saying Dad was a pig and Maggie saying if there wasn't a baby, Dad would come home. Janet ran to the window and looked inside. Dad had taken his coat off and laughed at something the blonde woman said, as if he hadn't just broken his daughter's heart. Unable to stand seeing him any longer, she pelted across the road and hid behind a car, waiting for…she didn't know what.

All she knew was she needed to stay there.

She wasn't sure how much time had passed, but later, the sky darkening with storm clouds, Dad and the woman left the pub. Dad pushed a bouncy Silver

Cross pram, the basket beneath full of presents wrapped in blue paper and cards propped beside them. Two shiny balloons on string bobbed from the handle. Janet watched them through the windows of a parked car until they reached the end of the street, then she followed.

It turned out Dad didn't live too far away from her and Mum. Three streets, which wasn't much, and it stung that he'd been so close all this time and she hadn't known. They went inside number sixteen, closing the green door behind them, and Janet stared at Dad's car, one she'd been in so many times.

"Let the tyres down," *Charlene said.* "That'll teach him."

It wasn't much, but it'd make Janet feel better, to get back at him for all the nasty things he'd said. She crouched by the rear tyre and unscrewed the cap, throwing it down the nearby drain.

"Come back another day and put a nail in the front tyre, and keep doing it so it really pisses him off," *Maggie suggested.*

"If I keep doing it, he'll catch me, might phone the police," Janet said.

"That's all right." *Charlene laughed.* "You can tell them he used to smack you. They'll put him in prison for it, and he won't get to see that new baby."

Maggie piped up. "There's a better way to make sure he doesn't see the baby."

Janet got up and ran home, blocking Maggie's voice out, the awful things she was still saying. She rushed round the back and burst into the kitchen, startling Mum who stood at the cooker taking a tray of roast potatoes out of the oven.

"What the devil's got into you, scaring me like that?" *Mum put the tray on a chopping board.*

Janet shut the door. "I saw Dad, he was in the pub, and he took me down the shop in the yard and said mean stuff to me." *Her eyes welled, and she burst out crying, running to her mother.*

Mum hugged her, stroking her hair with an oven-gloved hand, warm from the potato tray. "What did he say?"

"He said he didn't love me anymore and called me a fucking weirdo and to fuck off. He went to this house with a woman who has a baby and — "

"Did you follow him?" *Mum's stroking hand stilled.*

"Yeah, because Maggie wanted to know where he lives."

"Oh God. What did you do?"

"I let his back tyre down, Charlene told me to do it. I remembered, so that's good, isn't it?"

Mum laughed, surprising Janet.

"That's not funny. I shouldn't be laughing. You mustn't do anything like that again, all right?" Mum crouched and held Janet's hands. "Listen to me. If we want to keep Maggie and Charlene a secret, you can't see your dad. I've told him I'll sort it, I'll take care of everything with a doctor, but if he finds out I haven't, he's going to tell the social, like Irene would, do you understand?"

Janet nodded, fear pounding through her.

"I promised him I'd get you fixed. He thinks you're dangerous, love, and you scare him."

"But I don't mean to."

"I know."

"What if you take me to the doctor and I get better? Will he come home?"

"No, he's married to that lady now. Alice. Because he has a baby, it's too difficult for him to just leave her."

"He left me and you, so how come that wasn't difficult?"

"You'll understand more when you're bigger, but when a lady has a child, she loves it very much, and when her husband tries to get the child taken away, the mum tells him to leave because the baby is more important to her."

"Did you have to do that?"

"Yes."

"I don't like him anymore."

"Look, I only told him I'd take you to the doctor because he threatened to do it. I don't want you to be taken away from me, so we have to pretend you've been and you're all fixed, okay? Maybe Maggie and Charlene will leave you alone as you grow up. Lots of kids have pretend friends who disappear."

Janet kind of understood what Mum was saying. "You don't want me to go to that place where Mr Nasonova goes. Or to them nasty houses with other kids."

"No, and if your dad finds out I didn't stick to my promise, he'll make sure it happens. He thinks you're so naughty you don't belong at home with me. So please, so we can stay together, be a good girl outside of this house, okay? Be a good girl all the time if you can. One day, Maggie and Charlene will go, I promise, and everything will be all right."

"But what if it isn't and I hurt animals again? You said I did that."

Mum wiped Janet's tears away. "You did, but you didn't mean it, that's the main thing." She stood.

"Come on, get that coat and your wellies off. We'll have a nice Sunday dinner then play Monopoly, all right?"

Janet nodded. As she hung her coat up and put her wellies in the shoe rack, she told Maggie to stay away, that she didn't love her anymore, that she was a fucking weirdo and had to fuck off. It had hurt Janet when Dad had said it, enough for her to leave him alone, so maybe Maggie would be hurt enough to leave her alone, too.

Chapter Five

Janet arrived home and dumped her handbag on the hallway table. Mentally exhausted from her day, she kicked her high heels off, glad of the instant relief, and checked her post. A familiar-looking letter had arrived, and she rubbed her thumb over the back of the envelope, contemplating opening it now, then thought better of it. Best to leave it. She'd need to harden her heart to read those words, and she wasn't quite ready to slip into that persona. To let Charlene take care of the emotions Janet couldn't cope with.

She took the envelope into the kitchen and propped it against the bread bin where it seemed to glare at her, begging her to scan the contents. Shrugging off the silly thought, she sighed and pinched her wrist to centre herself. It reminded her of Dad pinching her there, and she gritted her teeth until it hurt so the pain eclipsed the memory.

At the fridge, she took out her trusty sweet white wine and poured a large measure—gone were the days where she'd have swigged it straight from the bottle before her pub crawls with Billie, the pair of them dancing while they got dolled up, ready to go on the prowl. She was better than that now, someone with standards. Or she appeared to be anyway. The truth was, she'd love to turn back time, return to before her major error with Sean and do things differently. With age came wisdom, and she'd have taken such a different route now. She'd have centred her experiment on removing Whitney, the woman who'd stood in her way. Why hadn't Janet seen that? Why had she targeted Emerald instead?

I was younger. Stupid. Desperate.

She got on with making dinner—cooking well was something she'd taught herself when she'd first had her eye on George as husband material. She'd needed the skill to lure him, basing her modus operandi on that saying: the way to a man's heart is through his stomach. Why then, hadn't she fed him chicken and mushroom Pot Noodles with buttered tiger bread? He'd have properly fallen for her, then.

And how thick of her to choose a man who was to all intents and purposes already married—to The Cardigan Estate and his brother. She'd been nothing but a mistress again and had known, deep down, she wouldn't be able to snag him, yet still she'd tried.

God loved a trier. And she was going to try again with him, too.

Chicken parmigiana baking in the oven—she couldn't be bothered with faffing about using the grill—she downed her remaining wine then went off for a shower. The bathroom had always been a place that unsettled her. Every time she saw white tiles she imagined them dripping with scarlet rivulets, and what with the letter waiting for her today, it brought old memories to the forefront.

A flash of the past swept across her vision—blood, screams, the tainted tiles, the red bathwater, those seventeen stab wounds. Most times she succeeded in pushing it all to the back of her mind, but with her visit to the prison tomorrow as well, she had to watch herself. Watch she didn't let that wine take her to places in her mind she'd managed to stop herself from examining too deeply. If she drank too much, she risked getting maudlin, picking everything apart and seeing her glaring mistakes. Plus there was a point of no return, she'd found, that edge she went too close to, when recklessness nudged her to step over, go into freefall, and see where it took her. Overdoing alcohol would zip her straight there.

"No," she shouted at the bath, at the water cascading from the showerhead, steam billowing. Or had she spoken to Charlene? "You will *not* make me go there. Never again. If I managed to get through the split with George without you, I can resist you. Now fuck off."

Insane laughter echoed in her head—was that *Maggie?*—and she squeezed her eyes shut while undressing. She knew exactly what that laughter meant. There she'd been, talking about resisting, but for a long time now she'd pondered on how to get rid of that person in prison. Maybe that was another, subconscious reason why she'd chosen George—because by the time he'd fallen so deeply for her, he'd have sorted out her issue. When George loved, he was in all the way and would do anything to make those he cared for happy.

"But he doesn't love you. If he did, he wouldn't mind you changing him. He'd want to please you, be whoever you want him to be."

She clenched her teeth at Charlene's voice. Fucking hell, this was so hard sometimes, fighting it, shoving off what she thought of as grasping hands desperate to drag her into that terrible pit where she was surrounded by empty wine bottles and the ghosts of her memories. If she succumbed, it would mean she'd have to struggle from scratch all over again. Rewrite her life all over again.

Under the stream of too-hot water, she imagined washing the sweat from those grasping

67

hands off her skin, soothing the scratches from the sharp nails. Once or twice, when delirious with alcohol, she'd *seen* those scratches as if they really existed, and bruises, so black and dark red, but they hadn't really been there. Nights had been full of delusion, where she hadn't known who the hell she was, voices clamouring to claim her mind as theirs. She'd been desperate to be the woman she was today, had cried and begged her other selves to free her.

And she'd won for a long time.

"You'll never win, Janet."

"Fuck. Off."

She concentrated on washing her hair, on her fingers massaging her scalp, taking herself down the imaginary steps to the beach. She listened to the sea crawling up the sand then retreating, the gulls calling to one another, the laughter of a little girl who ran along the sand, her hair streaming.

Five years old. Fingers sticky from an ice cream cone. Janet spying on the girl and her father, seething that Sean played happy families, albeit without the mother in tow.

Janet had ruined him.

Smug with that knowledge, she smiled. The battle within calmed, and she finished her shower, got dressed in her comfy leggings and oversized T-shirt, and returned to the kitchen. She microwaved a few prepacked new potatoes, some green beans, then dished up her chicken and sat on the sofa to eat.

How lonely this life was now without George in it of an evening. No more meals out, no more shows in the West End, ones he'd hated watching but had taken her to anyway—she'd been trying to recreate her time with Sean. Yes, George *had* cared, enduring the shows and even buying her tickets to one had proved that, but it was obvious why he'd wanted to end it. He didn't like not having control of his emotions, and she reckoned he'd been falling faster than he'd have liked. She'd sensed it coming, those hateful words where he'd sever their connection like Dad and Sean had, so she'd got there first, making out their relationship wasn't working. And truth be told, it wasn't. She'd tried to change him, to *save* him from himself, to get him on the right medication so he didn't suffer like she did, and he'd seen it as her needing to remove his control.

Back in the kitchen, she swilled her plate, stacked it in the dishwasher, and poured another glass of wine. *Make this the last one, Janet.* She took the letter into the living room and put it on the seat cushion beside her. Stared at it for a while. Braced herself to see things in her mind she didn't want to see, to remember, to experience the emotions she had back when she'd hung around with the person who'd written to her. There was no question of letting that person go, of allowing them to rot away in prison without Janet keeping an eye on them. She had to know their thoughts, what their plans were, so she could act accordingly.

"Kill her, it's the only way to keep the secret safe."

Wine gone, Janet slid her finger beneath the envelope flap and took the paper out. It was A4, folded into thirds, and she shrugged off the fact someone else had read it before it had been sent to her. Someone checking for code words, hidden messages, or whatever the hell the prison service looked out for. They probably wouldn't find much apart from the sender bleating the same old rubbish—they hadn't committed the crime, they were innocent, someone had framed them. Officers must read that tripe all the time and ignore it. Besides, the evidence said different. They *weren't* innocent. They *did* deserve to spend twenty years banged up.

That evidence was manufactured, a big fat lie.

She opened the paper out. One page, filled with that small, blocky penmanship, as though Billie wanted to fit as much in as she could. So it was going to be one of *those* letters, then. Rambling.

Dear Janet,

I know I've said this before, but I seriously can't do this anymore. I'm at the end of my road. For sure this time. There's only so much that innocent, incarcerated people can take. The unfairness of it is what's always got me. People who knew me then, they know damn well I don't have it in me to kill someone. I mean, really? Those who believe I could do that, well, they're deluded. I know, I know, there was the evidence, blah, blah, blah, but for God's sake! All that crap about me going into some kind of state—what was it they said? A fugue. It's rubbish. I know what you're thinking, that if I can't remember doing it, I must have been in a fugue, but…

There's no point in me going over the murder again with you. I'm actually sick of talking about it. Getting on my own nerves. No one except Freda believes me anyway, and that's only because she didn't kill anyone either so understands how I feel. Even you think I did

71

it, and you're my best friend. At least you stuck by me, though. No one else has. I still can't believe my mum ditched me, acting like I'm some kind of monster.

As for the drugs, I don't remember taking them, I swear. Who gave them to me? Can you remember now? You said in court you couldn't, but you've had time to think. You were at the party, I was with you, so how could you not have seen something? Oh yeah, I forgot. I supposedly went to the bathroom, did the murder, then came back with blood all over me. And what normal person reappears with the obvious evidence on them that they've killed someone? You've even said yourself that the natural response is to panic, to cover it up, to remove yourself from the scene.

It's that bad sometimes, to get to the truth, I imagine someone putting the LSD in my drink. It's the only plausible explanation. Someone at that fucking party framed me. And that blood... When I came to, you know, after, and smelled it... You'll never know how revolting that was. It had dried, was under my fingernails and everything. Sorry, you know all this. It just helps to write it out, the shit in my head. For as long as I live, I'll never shut up about being innocent. If I did, that would make people think I'm guilty, that I've finally realised no one's going to believe me so I may as well accept the blame. How could I, though?

Who the hell would admit to something they haven't done?

I know what you're thinking, that ending things is another way of admitting guilt. I can't remember doing it, and that's true, I can't, but I know it inside me, I wouldn't have done something so hideous, not to a little girl. She didn't deserve what happened to her.

This woman, she's in for murder as well, and she said I'm in denial, that because I can't remember, I'm telling myself it didn't happen because the guilt of it would be too much. I can see her point, and she said allowing myself to admit it would mean I'd have a more peaceful life, then I could ask the family for forgiveness, but I can't do it. Unless I see video evidence of me actually using that knife, I'll never believe it.

Anyway, I feel better now for getting it down on paper, and sorry, yet again, for putting you through having to read this. Once, I wondered whether you really do read my letters, but you always talk about what's in them on the visits, so I told myself off for thinking nasty things. This place, it sends you mad, takes you into these really deep wells in your head, and you're stuck down at the bottom, and it's too hard to get out. It makes you think stuff you shouldn't.

I did what you said on your last visit and joined the therapy group. The man who comes in and runs it is all right. Jerry Landers. Do you know him? Loads of women fancy him, but he's not a patch on you when it comes to helping me. When you visit me, I'm okay for about two weeks afterwards. You have a great way of making me see things differently. Him, though… I can tell he looks down his nose at us, know what I mean? Like he's only doing a job, he doesn't really care about us. Thinks we're scum. He's ticking the boxes. Making himself look good for whoever.

He's married. Wears a silver wedding ring. It doesn't stop people from flirting with him, though. I find that rude, don't you? Like he's a sex object. It's uncomfortable to watch them being gross with him, like he'd fancy them back or something. Freda reckons he'll lose his temper soon. She says she's noticed his jaw clenching when all the inuendoes come out. Can't say I blame him if he snaps at someone, but a part of me thinks if he doesn't like the situation, he shouldn't come to help us. Like, why does he keep putting himself through it?

Can't you apply for his job? You'd be so much better than him.

Here's a bit of drama. This newbie came in last week. A strange sort, kind of jumpy at dinner, kept her head down, like I did when I first got here. I could tell she was scared to look at anyone in case they beat the shit out of her for it. She apparently killed her baby, so yeah, she was right to keep off the radar. Anyway, she was only here for one night, then they found her, if you catch my drift. Said she'd done it to herself, but some of us think otherwise. Rumours, they get around. I'm surprised no one's done that to me yet. No one here likes a kid killer.

It got me thinking about doing the same thing — doing it first before someone else can bump me off. I've been lucky to be left alone all this time as it is and even luckier that Freda gives me the time of day. I'm laughing, because once whoever reads this before you, I'll probably be put on watch. Monitored. I mean, what does it matter if I use a sheet like she did? Apart from you and Freda, there's no one who'd give a fuck whether I was gone anyway.

Bollocks, someone's here to take me to the therapy group, so I'd better go. Looking forward to the next visit so much, even if it's only me saying goodbye. I might have the balls to do 'it' by then. One less drain on the prison system, eh?

See you soon.

Love you,

Billie

Janet sighed. It would be easier if Billie did away with herself. It'd solve the problem of Janet always worrying about the truth finally getting out. In the past, she'd encouraged Billie to see the brighter side, that just because she was in prison, it didn't mean she couldn't find happiness. Janet secretly enjoyed seeing Billie's life play out inside, how Janet's would have played out had she confessed to what she'd done. Even though Billie had committed the murder, she didn't really deserve to be there.

Janet did.

Still, if she didn't go through with her plan to have Billie offed, and Billie didn't use the sheet, her friend had things she could look forward to. There were books to lose herself in, and she could study, ready for when she got out. She had so much time to get her ducks in a row before her release in fifteen or so years. Aim for a brand-new life. Although Janet didn't much like the idea of Billie latching on to her on the outside.

With Billie so obviously down, now might be the right time to encourage her to end it all instead of Janet getting the twins involved. If only she could get away with taking Billie to The Place of Stillness, coaxing her down the steps to the beach and planting another seed on the visit tomorrow. It would look weird, though, to the officers watching, Billie sitting there with her eyes shut while Janet whispered to her. Billie had mentioned suicide in her letter, so wouldn't they automatically think she'd planned this for a while and write it off as just another guilty person unable to accept what they'd done? They wouldn't think for one moment that Janet had planted the seed, just like they hadn't when Billie had killed that child.

Janet shouldn't be thinking like this. She'd promised herself she wouldn't go down this road again.

"It's the best road, Janet, you know that."

"I'm not listening."

"Who are you kidding? You're always *listening to me."*

Janet got up, taking the letter into her bedroom and putting it in the box with all the others. They were trophies, those A4 pieces of paper, something she kept to remind her of the power she'd wielded, how she'd influenced a woman to indulge herself in one of the worst sins.

"Do not murder, do not commit adultery, do not steal, do not bear false witness," Jesus had supposedly said. *Matthew 19:18*.

Billie had murdered, and Janet had aided in adultery, stolen Billie's freedom, and borne false witness, lying under oath. It had to be done, though. Just a shame Charlene had used Billie to get what she wanted.

A shame, too, that it hadn't worked out the way she'd hoped.

Chapter Six

The baby wasn't breathing anymore.

Alice had left it in the pram outside the shop, tucked into the alleyway beside it. How trusting. Mind you, so many people around here did that, some going as far as to park prams outside pubs and go inside to get pissed, only collecting the baby when someone came in and said it was screaming. That was bad mothering, Maggie reckoned. So why had Dad gone with someone like her? Mum would never let a baby out of her sight. She was worth a million of this Alice bitch.

With gloves on, Maggie had crammed a scrunched-up carrier bag in the baby's little mouth—as much of it as she could anyway—pushing it right into the throat. Now Dad could come home. It wouldn't be difficult anymore, it would be simple with no other child to worry about. Janet could have him back, and that was all that mattered, wasn't it? Janet kept saying she didn't want him back anymore because he'd been nasty to her, but she was lying. She wouldn't still cry for him at night otherwise.

Maggie skipped down the alley in the February sunshine on this Saturday afternoon, stopping at the end to look down another cobbled alley that ran behind the shops and houses. Sometimes, boys played football there, and she didn't want to get caught leaving the scene of the crime. Coast clear, she dodged rubbish bins and scooted round a pile of dog shit, coming out at the playing field bordering the park. She ran into the thick bundle of trees that surrounded it, walking the edge of the area to see who was about, to catch her breath. She didn't want to get Janet into trouble for what she'd just done, so no one was allowed to see her until she wanted them to.

She needed an alibi—Mum had told Janet what one of those was in case they had to lie to anyone in the future about her whereabouts and behaviour.

Three quarters of the way round, Maggie stopped behind a wide tree trunk and peered round it. She watched the kids playing on the swings, two boys kicking a football on the grass. If she timed it right, when they were all facing away from her, she could appear nonchalantly and no one would be any the wiser as to where she'd been before now. Billie was on the roundabout, spinning fast, and Maggie went to the edge of the trees on the opposite side of where she'd entered. She stepped onto the short path that joined the grass to the nearby street as if she'd come from that direction, then headed towards the kids.

Billie looked across and waved, slowing the roundabout with her foot. "Didn't think you were coming."

"Mum's gone to the bingo with yours, so..." Maggie scuffed her shoe on the asphalt. "Want to get some sweets up the shop?"

Billie dipped her head. "Got no money."

"I have."

Maggie took the fiver out of her pocket, the one she'd stolen from Alice's purse that had been in the handbag under the pram. The silly cow had taken a tenner from *it before going in the shop, leaving the rest of the spoils behind.*

"Where did you get that?" Billie stared, mouth open, eyes wide.

"Found it on the way here."

"Talk about lucky. We'll get loads of stuff with that."

Maggie smiled. "Sweets, crisps, some pop. Come on."

They ran hand in hand across the grass. In the cobbled alley, Maggie veered left and slowed, Billie gasping at the sight of a copper at the end of the other alley beside the shop. Maggie didn't care about the police, she didn't think she had anything to worry about, so tugged her friend along.

The policeman shook his head. "You'll need to go the other way." He pointed behind them.

"Aww! We just want to go to the shop," Maggie said.

"Yep, like I said, the other way."

"What's gone on?" she asked.

"None of your business."

Maggie wanted to tell him he should be questioning her, should do his job properly, but he'd already dismissed them, staring to his left, probably keeping an eye on the dead kid in the pram.

She had to stop herself from laughing.

They turned and headed down to the next alley a few metres ahead, houses and their back gardens either side of it.

"Wonder why we can't go down there?" Billie skipped, excitement written all over her.

"Dunno." Maggie didn't know whether she should act excited, too. Was it weird that she didn't seem bothered? What would Janet do and say? "Maybe there's been a big robbery with guns and stuff, and Mr Balakrishnan's been shot. That'd serve him right. He always watches us whenever we're in there, like we're going to nick things."

"D'you reckon that's what's happened?" Billie slapped a hand over her mouth.

"It might have. Why else would a copper be guarding the alley?"

"Bloody hell," Billie said and laughed because she'd used a swear word.

They came out into the street where the shop was and took a left. Police cars and an ambulance were up the road, and coppers in uniform stood at front doors opposite the shop. People had come out to nose. Women with handknitted cardigans double-wrapped over their middles, still with their slippers on where they'd been so eager to get outside and had forgotten to switch for shoes. Children messing about around their legs, bored. Men with roll-ups stuck to their bottom lips, squinting across to see what all the fuss was about and, so likely for these parts, thanking their lucky stars the coppers weren't here for them, coming to arrest them for hooky gear. It would be the same if it had happened in Janet's street. Irene next door would be the first to come storming out to get a front-row spot.

Billie clutched Maggie's hand tighter. "Something bad must have happened. There's an ambulance, so Mr Balakrishnan must have got shot."

"Probably. You know what it's like round here."

Maggie bravely led the way, stopping short beside a beige Mini. Alice came streaking out of the alley, screaming, blonde hair flying. Noisy bitch. Maggie glanced to her left. In the alley, ambulance people stepped back from the baby on a blanket on the ground. They must have tried to save it. What was the point? The bloody thing hadn't been breathing when Maggie had left it. The officer at the other end hung his head, as if he cared that the kid had snuffed it, which was well weird, because Maggie wouldn't care if a stranger had died. Maybe you were supposed to pretend you gave a shit when you were a policeman.

Alice ran out into the road, into the arms of a woman, the one she'd sat with in the Sickle. The possible sister.

"That's your dad's wife," Billie whispered urgently, tugging on Maggie's arm. "The one I told you about. Blimey, is that her baby? It's gone a funny colour."

Maggie shrugged. "Looks like her kid got hurt. Maybe the robbers bashed it over the head or something."

"There's no blood, though."

"Shame."

"It's not a shame. I don't like blood."

Maggie pushed into the shop.

A policeman approached them. "Before you get your mitts on anything, where have you been?"

"Up the park," Billie said. "Ask that other copper down the alley. He saw us coming from there."

"Oh, I will do. Did anyone see you there?" he asked.

"Karen Bayley and her sisters were on the swings." Billie glanced to the ceiling, thinking. "Oh, and Mark Rotherby and Scott Jones playing footy."

He nodded. "Right, and what's your names?"

Billie told them. Maggie was too fascinated watching Alice through the shop window to provide the answer. Alice pulled at her hair and screamed to the sky, her eyes bulging. Silly cow. Why get upset about a baby who was nothing but a pest? It had been a pain in the arse just for being alive.

"Right," the plod said. "Hurry up and buy your things, then go home. No nicking."

"We don't need to nick," Billie said. "Janet's got money, so there."

Maggie snapped out of her staring to go to the sweet section and pick up her favourites. "Two-fifty each. I'll share the whole fiver."

"All right. Ta."

Mr Balakrishnan eyed them as they went up to the counter. As usual, he craned his neck to see if their jacket pockets bulged. He seemed content they weren't stealing and rang up their goodies. Maggie wished there had been a robbery and he'd got shot. The stupid old man got on her nerves.

They paid and left, dawdling along the street scoffing Twixes, Maggie pleased she'd killed that kid. She'd fixed things for Janet, and everything would be all right now.

On the roundabout at the park, Janet stared at the sweet and crisp wrappers, the empty cans of pop twitching in the breeze. Something had happened. That sinking feeling she'd come to understand— Maggie had been inside her. Something awful had gone on, she just knew it. She couldn't ask Billie what it was, how they'd got the money to pay for all this stuff, nor could she ask why she was at the park when she'd told Billie she wasn't going. If she asked, "Did I do something naughty?" Billie would think she was crackers.

Frightened, unsure what to think or say, Janet bit her lip and, inside her head, asked Maggie what she'd done.

Silence.

"I reckon that baby's definitely dead." Billie picked their rubbish up. "Did you see it? All blue round the mouth and stuff."

Baby? Dead? Janet's heart pounded too hard. "Yeah."

Billie ran off to put their rubbish in the bin then got back on the roundabout. "Must be weird for you cos it's your brother."

"I don't know him, but if he's dead, that's got to be sad for his mum." That was the sort of thing she was expected to say, but the shock of her baby brother not being alive anymore had her feeling sick. She didn't want him around, and she'd wished he'd disappear, had even thought about him dying, but she wouldn't have done anything about it.

Maggie must have been listening to Janet's thoughts. Why wasn't Charlene telling her what had happened? Why had both of them gone into hiding, leaving Janet to flounder on her own? She hated it when they did that after a bad event. It was like they didn't want to get into trouble at the same time she did.

"And it'd be horrible for your dad, don't forget," Billie reminded her.

Janet didn't care if Dad was upset. He deserved it after what he'd done to her and Mum. She struggled for what to ask, how to get information without revealing she didn't have a clue what was going on. Every part of her had gone cold, and she was scared of the police. It was as if she knew they were involved during her blackout somehow. A sixth sense. Or maybe Maggie hadn't hidden the memory from her well enough and that bit still lingered.

"Wonder what was wrong with it to just die like that?" Billie said. "It wasn't a robbery, else we'd have heard the neighbours talking about it when we left the shop. Alice must have gone in there if the pram was down the alley. We should have asked that copper."

So they had been near a policeman.

Janet fought to remember but couldn't. "I expect I'll find out when I get home. Mum will know, or your mum will. They'll have already been told at the bingo, I bet." It amazed her how quickly news spread in their corner of the world.

"Yeah, we should go back now. Mum said I had to be home before her." Billie clambered off the roundabout and waited for Janet to join her. "Ugh, I ate too many sweets. I feel sick."

Janet felt sick for another reason.

Billie's eyes lit up. "Let's go and see if there's more money where you found that fiver."

What? A sinking feeling dragged Janet down. She walked to the pathway that led to the street. She didn't know anything about a fiver, she'd assumed Billie had pocket money which was why they'd pigged out on sweets. It scared her to have a chunk of her day missing. The last thing she remembered was Billie coming to her house, asking her to go to the park, Janet saying no, then being on the roundabout. She'd definitely scoffed her head off because she still tasted the salt and vinegar from the crisps.

"Where was it?" Billie asked.

Janet stared at her, confused again. "Where was what?"

"The fiver!"

"Oh, over here." Janet went to a lamppost at the end of the road and made a show of looking for more cash. The grass around it was so long she had to move the blades with her shoe. "There's nothing here."

"Poo. Never mind." Billie linked arms and guided Janet towards their street. "It must have died in its sleep or something, that baby."

"Yeah."

"It was on the telly about it, how that sometimes happens. Something about being asleep on their bellies, I dunno. They just fall asleep and don't wake up."

"That's horrible."

Halfway down, women gathered at Irene's weathered front gate. News must have spread. It wasn't surprising, but it bugged Janet that everyone else knew something she didn't. Irene was the one to either make or break people who moved into his road. If she didn't like you, that was it, she set up a campaign to get rid of you. Mum was constantly worried she'd turn on her, but so far, Irene had only stuck to snide comments and threats.

"She's nagging, as usual," Billie muttered. "My mum's scared of her, you know. Says Irene's a bully with a long reach, whatever that means."

"It'll be the graffiti gang," Janet said.

"Yeah."

No one wanted to wake up with nasty words spray-painted on their front door, but Irene made it happen if she fell out of favour with anyone. Janet was surprised she hadn't done it to theirs yet, seeing as she mumbled stuff about grassing Mum up to social services.

They went closer to the gossiping gaggle, and Janet wished Mum was home so she could tell her she'd had another blackout. She checked her watch. Bingo didn't finish for another hour.

"Murdered, so I heard," Irene said loudly, as if she wanted to scare Janet and Billie.

"Murdered?" Mrs Robins said, late to the party, having just run over the road to join in. "Who's been murdered?"

"A baby," Irene said. "Someone stuffed a carrier bag, of all things, in the poor little mite's mouth while it was in its pram down the shop alley. We've all done that, left our kiddies, haven't we, but never once have we thought it would get killed. What's the world coming to?"

"Or this area," Mrs Robins said.

Janet's legs went wobbly, and she clutched Billie's arm tighter. "Murdered?" she whispered.

"God," Billie said. "That's horrible, that is. I've gone all goosebumpy."

Janet tried hard to keep the sick down. "What's happened?" she asked Irene, needing the woman to repeat the story.

"Oh, well, it's best you find out from your mother."

"We already know," Billie said. "We were at the park then went to the shop, and Alice's baby was dead."

"So it is true, then," old Mrs Fort said.

"Of course it's fucking true," Irene barked. "Do you think I'd make something like that up? Our Maureen rang, she lives opposite the shop, and she told me. She's had coppers at her door and everything." She stared at Janet. "Are you all right?" It sounded like she pretended to care.

Janet shrugged.

Irene mouthed "weirdo" at Mrs Fort. "Anyway, I can't stand here gossiping all day, I've got things to do."

"Like smoking at her table," Maggie said.

Janet almost jumped at hearing the voice. Worried Maggie would take over and say or do something, she blurted, "I'd better go. See you later, Billie."

She ran into the back garden and took the key out from under the rock, opened the door, and put the key back. She locked herself in using the other key on a hook *by the cupboard with the teabags in it and rushed to her bedroom, tears hot. Scared out of her mind, she threw herself onto her bed and sobbed, wishing she was someone else who didn't have a Maggie or a Charlene inside them.*

"What did you do?" she said into her pillow.

"Fixed things," *Maggie said.* "Dad will come back now, you wait and see."

Janet sat up, her hair stuck to her wet cheek. Hot, she took her gloves and coat off. "Did...did you m-make me kill that b-baby?"

Oh God, what if someone had seen her doing it like they had with the animals? What if the police came round? What if she was taken away and put into a kid prison or something? No one other than Mum would believe her if she said Maggie had done it. Dad had stopped loving her because of Maggie. What if Mum did that, too, if she'd murdered that kid?

She flopped onto her back and closed her eyes, shaking, so frightened. She lay there for a long time, tears flowing, so many things floating through her head, Maggie and Charlene silent, leaving her to deal with this by herself. She was a nasty person, as bad as them, because a part of her was pleased the baby was dead. Dad shouldn't get to love it when he already had her. He shouldn't be allowed to forget her like he had.

93

It didn't even make sense. He'd loved her before he'd left. He'd been so kind. Or was that something she'd told herself so she didn't get upset, so she didn't have to face the fact he'd smacked her?

Had she always been weird and he'd pretended to care about her, then when it had got bad, he'd walked out? Why had he wanted to leave Mum, though? It wasn't her fault Janet did naughty things.

"Don't you remember the row the night before?" *Charlene asked.* "He said he was sick of Mum sticking up for you and couldn't hack it anymore. He said she cared more about you than him."

The memory came back. Mum's raised voice from downstairs. Dad sounding calm, although he did swear. A lot.

"She's not right in the fucking head," he'd said. "I shit myself whenever she goes into one of her moods. The way she stares at me, it's like she's possessed. I'm actually scared of her, my own child. I'm frightened of a bloody kid! She needs help."

"I won't have you saying things like that about her. If you're making me choose, I'll choose her every time."

"Do something about her. If you don't, I will."

The door had slammed.

"Remember?" *Maggie said.* "That's why we have to hurt him. He said horrible things about us. People who upset us have to learn the hard way by paying for what they've done."

"The baby didn't hurt us," Janet said.

Maggie didn't reply.

The sound of the key going in the lock on the front door had Janet scooting down the stairs, so relieved she could spill her terrible secret. "Mum. Mum!"

"What's the matter?" Mum paused halfway into the kitchen, her handbag dangling from the crook of her arm.

"The baby's dead. I went out and didn't know. I was on the roundabout up the park, and Billie said he was dead."

"Oh, Jesus Christ. What baby?"

"Dad's!"

Mum closed her eyes and leant on the doorjamb. Her bag dropped to the floor. Her lips trembled, and she went pale, same as she had just before she'd been sick that time she'd drunk too much gin after Dad had left them.

She opened her eyes. "Maggie?"

Janet ran to her and cuddled her around the waist. "It wasn't me, I promise it wasn't me."

Mum's hand came to rest on Janet's head. "Tell me everything you remember, all right? Then I'll sort your alibi."

Chapter Seven

I chabod woke at eight in the morning, although he remained slumped down in the driver's seat of the Saab. He hadn't intended to sleep here overnight, but just after twelve a.m., his eyelids had drooped, and he'd zipped his coat up for warmth, telling himself he'd just have forty winks. He'd had a few thousand by the looks of it, his eyes gritty, a crick in his neck from sleeping upright, head resting on the window.

He'd kill for one of Debbie's coffees.

He soon perked up without the caffeine, though. Janet came out of her place holding a carrier bag, her face devoid of the usual makeup, and got in her car. She wasn't dressed for work, no sharp, snappy skirt suit, instead opting for jeans, a pink T-shirt, and a cerise fleece jacket. He hadn't had her down as a pink person, more the corporate greys and blacks of a no-nonsense businesswoman. Maybe she was nipping to the shop round the corner for some milk or whatever. She might even get ready at the office later. She probably had her fancy clothes in that bag.

He stared in surprise. She put her hair up in a bun then jammed a black, short wig over her head. It changed her dramatically. She slid dark-framed glasses on and checked herself in the rearview mirror.

Reminds me of that comedienne, Sue Perkins.

What the feck is she up tae?

He quickly sent the twins a message.

ICH: SHE'S ON THE MOVE. GOT A DISGUISE ON. WILL FOLLOW IN CAR.

He took a picture of her then sent it to them. What would they make of it? Did they know she dressed up sometimes? Their lack of letting him know all the details was detrimental at a time like this, but it wasn't like he could rake them over the coals for it, was it?

No reply came, so he peeled out of his parking spot and tailed her.

It became clear she was leaving London, and his curiosity level went higher. Where was she going? And why did she need to go there in that getup?

An hour later, having kept back two car lengths on the A road, he got his answer. She turned into a prison car park, and he kept going, finding a space down the road, pointing his vehicle towards the entrance so he could see her coming back out.

ICH: SHE'S VISITING SOMEONE AT HIS MAJESTY'S PLEASURE.

GG: GOT TO BE THE FRIEND. JUST SEEN YOUR OTHER MESSAGE AND THE PIC. WHAT THE FUCKING, WANKING, BASTARD SHIT IS SHE PLAYING AT, PUTTING A DISGUISE ON?

ICH: DISGUISES EQUAL SUSPICION IN MY BOOK. SHE LOOKS REALLY DIFFERENT, TOO. I WOULDN'T

HAVE KNOWN IT WAS HER IF I HADN'T SEEN HER PUT THE WIG ON.

GG: KEEP FOLLOWING HER.

Ichabod settled down to wait. In his experience, she could be a good while in there, all those security checks, the visit itself, then another check on the way out. He was still tired but didn't dare nap. He didn't have a death wish, and if he missed her reappearance and the twins found out, he'd be dead meat.

Chapter Eight

An hour after her arrival, Janet sat at a table that reminded her of being at school, wide enough for two chairs side by side, only here, they were also opposite, and there were four all told. She supposed that was in case someone had more than one visitor at the same time, which wasn't unheard of, considering husbands came with kids or a convict's mother minded the grandchildren on the outside until the day they could be handed back over to their mums. Some would never again take charge of their little ones, though, in here for too long, and when they got out, the youngsters would be adults.

All very sobering. All very stupid of them to commit crime themselves instead of manipulating someone else to do it for them. But it was none of Janet's business what the other women had done or how their worlds had changed from their lack of foresight and planning. All she concerned herself with was Billie and how *that* particular killer's behaviour affected her.

The visiting room, awash with people anxious or eager to see their loved ones, had various layers of smells in the air. It was again similar to school, like a dining hall, row upon row of tables, and at the end, a hatch where you could buy tea, coffee, and treats. There was another room, so Billie had said, different to this one in looks and atmosphere, used by the more dangerous prisoners who needed Perspex between them and whoever had come to sit and a chat.

A door at the far end opened, and the incarcerated women filed in, grey tracksuits that matched the pallor of their skin singling them out as wrongdoers, faces a myriad of expressions: foreheads furrowed through fear of who they'd encounter, perhaps a unwanted visitor; eyebrows arched in expectation of seeing a much-loved person; bottom lips clamped between teeth, anxiety high; but most of all, smiles and sparkling eyes, and that slump of the shoulders that occurred with the relief of, "You're here! Oh God, you came!"

Billie didn't have any of that. Face blank, as though no emotion lived inside her, shoulders up by her ears, she hugged her skinny frame and trudged forward, pale-blonde hair cut into a severe, jaw-length bob with a sideswept fringe which she'd tucked behind her ear. It needed a good wash, and she had the air about her that she ought to use deodorant. She appeared unwashed, her skin clammy.

What had happened to: *Looking forward to the next visit so much?* Why was she so upset? *...even if it's only me saying goodbye.* That had to be it. Was she dreading speaking to Janet for the last time? Was she still in that mindset? Or was her sour façade because she'd gone the other way, once again determined to prove she was innocent?

Janet sighed. It would be a long, boring visit if it was the latter, and honestly, she wasn't in the mood to go over and over the past with her.

Billie sat and, still with her arms wrapped across her middle, she leant forward and whispered, "Like I thought they would, they've put me on bloody watch, so expect to be stared at the whole bloody time you're here."

Janet smiled kindly. What she wanted to say was: *Well, when you go on about using a sheet to top yourself, what do you expect?* Instead, she offered, "But you knew they would, love, you said that in your letter, didn't you?"

"I know, but I'm getting desperate. Like, I *really* want to do it this time, then in the next breath I don't, but there's no point in me carrying on, trying to do a sodding uni course when, after I get out, no one would want to employ me anyway. Not when they know about…*that*."

"They'd only know if you told them."

"Most do background checks, so it'd come up. That's why I can't return to nursing. All those years of study, wasted."

"I could ask my friends to give you a job. They won't mind what happened so long as you're sorry for it." Janet had no intention of tapping the twins up years down the line and asking them to help Billie out because it'd mean answering questions: *How do you know her? Why are you still mates with a kid killer? How do we know she won't do it again? Are you fucking mental, expecting us to employ someone like that? Knob right off.*

Billie's cynical laugh cut across the surrounding chatter. "I can't believe you call people like that 'friends'."

"Well, they are."

Billie shook her head. "Weird how life takes us places we never thought we'd go, isn't it? Me in here, you out there mingling with gangsters. Who'd have predicted it?"

"I don't mingle, I work for them."

Janet hadn't told her about seeing George in a romantic capacity. Billie would say she was rubbing it in, that Janet was busy loving life while she couldn't. Explaining wasn't worth the hassle, and how *could* she explain that she'd been using George, and all of her clients, to try to fix herself? Billie didn't know Janet even had a mental health problem. She wasn't aware Janet was a basket case and did a damn good job of hiding it.

"Whatever." Billie let out a long breath. "Anyway, I have to keep reminding myself it's not all doom and gloom. I've got one last try at something, and if that goes tits up, *then* I'll *do it*."

Janet didn't like the sound of this. "A last try at what?"

Billie eyed the hatch up. "Are you going to get me a coffee and bit of cake then or what?"

While Janet battled with anger at Billie not answering her question, she smiled to mask it and left the table, joining the queue. Only two people stood ahead of her, everyone else having bought the goodies before the prisoners had appeared. She bought them both a coffee and chose a jam doughnut and a slice of carrot cake, both for Billie. At first, Janet had always made out she didn't want hers so Billie got extra, but Billie now took it for granted she got two treats.

Janet carried her purchases back to the table on a tray and set everything out.

Billie bit into the cake and closed her eyes. Janet studied her, wishing she'd choke on a clump and die. It would certainly put a full stop at the end of that particular story.

Billie had aged since last month, as if worry wrinkles had sprouted in abundance. The dark shadows beneath her eyes spoke of sleepless nights, and the brackets around her mouth had got deeper, probably all that pursing of the lips she did. Janet didn't feel anything with regards to having put Billie in this position—no remorse. A shame, because they'd been such good friends as kids. Charlene had put paid to Janet having any kind of guilt trip. Billie had done what Charlene had needed her to, she'd been a tool and nothing more, and Janet had accepted that. Kind of like that saying, where people came into your life for a season. Granted, they'd known each other for their spring and summer years, and at one time Janet would have thought they'd be thick as thieves throughout their autumn and winter, too, but no. Better that Billie was the one scoffing carrot cake in confinement than Janet.

Slice gone, Billie attacked the sugar-covered doughnut then sipped her coffee. Janet did the same, asking herself if this was going to be one of those visits where Billie barely said a word and it was a waste of time coming.

To chivvy her friend into talking, Janet said, "How's Freda?"

Billie glanced across at the older woman two rows over with a number four haircut, grey with white at the temples, and a thick, gnarled scar from the edge of one nostril down to her top lip.

Someone in here had sliced her face open in a fight having taken exception to her murdering an old woman at the care home she'd worked at. Freda was supposedly innocent, too.

"Aren't they all," Charlene said. *"Losers."*

Billie made eye contact with Janet. "That's the last try I was on about. Freda said I should apply to the Crown Court for permission to appeal, seeing as I didn't do it after I was sentenced. I was too fucked up with shock back then."

"How can you do that? The twenty-eight days are long passed for you to be allowed down that route. The time to do that was five years ago."

"Like I don't know that. *I'm* the one serving the sentence, remember. I'm reminded of it the whole time I'm awake, and I sometimes dream about it an' all. Christ, you can be so insensitive sometimes." Billie licked sugar from the corner of her mouth. "I *can* do it once I've got proof of new evidence."

Janet's stomach lurched. "And how will you get that?"

"Freda's mates with someone who knows a private investigator."

Fucking hell. Janet hid her irritation, her anger, her fear. Having someone snooping around again wasn't what she needed. PIs had a habit of going further, digging deeper. "Who is this person? Are they reputable?"

"Of course they are."

"And how are you going to pay for it?"

"Freda said he'll wait for me to pay him after, like when I get money off the government or wherever for being wrongly convicted."

He sounded like an incompetent twat if he was prepared to do that for someone he didn't even know, and Janet could only hope he was. If he spun lines like that, he must be thick up top. Who worked with no guarantee of being paid?

"But you weren't wrongly convicted," Janet reminded her gently.

"God, burst my bubble, why don't you."

"Sorry, I didn't mean to do that, it's just you need to face facts. I don't want you going into this thinking you're going to be exonerated."

Billie sniffed.

Janet had better make a show of trying to help. "Has he got a name so I can check him out for you?"

For the first time since she'd come in, Billie seemed happy. "Would you?"

"Yes. I can get my friends to look into him, too, if you want, make sure he's kosher. Not being funny, but you don't know Freda that well, not really, not like you do me, and she could be having you on."

Billie glanced at Freda again. "I suppose. I did wonder, when she first made friends, whether she'd been sent by *that* family to get the truth out of me."

That family was the Dobsons, the parents of the child Billie had stabbed to death.

"Why would they know someone like her, though?" Janet asked. "As in, they're not people who're in the know like that. They're not the type to be able to pick up the phone and ring someone dodgy to help them out."

"Must be paranoia talking on my part," Billie said. "Happens a lot in here."

"Poor you." Janet didn't reach out to pat Billie's hand. While it was relaxed in here in most respects, touching wasn't allowed except for children hugging mums hello and goodbye, and even then it was brief, the officers keeping a beady eye out for any exchanges. Drugs. Razor blades. Money. Tiny mobile phones.

Billie picked at a spot on her cheek. "Anyway, you were the one who brought up Freda maybe having me on."

"She might have suggested an investigator so you'd definitely *stick around* as her friend."

"Stick around?" Billie frowned. "It's not like I can fucking go anywhere, is it."

"No, I mean…" Janet lowered her voice. "Did you tell her about using the sheet?"

"Ah, I get you. She's trying to stop me from doing it."

"Yes, and by bringing up a PI, it gives you enough hope to keep living. Maybe she's got used to being your buddy and would miss you if you weren't here."

"But that doesn't make sense, her lying. I'd be waiting for him to visit me, to discuss everything. I'd soon know if he didn't really exist, so he must do."

Janet drank more coffee. "So what are you expecting him to do, talk to everyone who was at the party?" The thought of that fired up her ever-present, simmering rage. The fact he'd get to speak to Sean when she couldn't… It irked the shit out of her. She'd been banned from Sean's life, sent scuttling away, made to feel ashamed of what had been between them, when before the murder, he'd been happy enough to take the sex and free counselling on offer.

"It's a place to start," Billie said. "Jerry, the therapy bloke, said people repress memories out of shock, which is why I asked you if you remembered if someone had given me that LSD. A few people might recall stuff now time has passed." She shrugged. "It's worth a try."

"It is." *It bloody isn't*. Annoyed things weren't going the way she wanted—the way Charlene wanted them to go by Billie using that sheet once she was off the watch—she faked a smile. "Unusual for someone to take payment based on money that might not materialise, though. He's got to be an angel or something, a bloke who's more interested in righting wrongs than making a living. And the court might refuse an appeal. Or if you get another trial, you might get found guilty again. Then what?"

"Are you deliberately raining on my parade?"

"What? No! I'm just making you aware there might be disappointment down the road, that's all. I'd hate for you to get your hopes so high, then have them crushed. Let me check the man out first before you agree to anything, okay? You didn't give me his name."

"He's called Randy Baker."

Janet held back a choke of laughter. "Um, what?"

Billie frowned again. "Oh God. She *is* having me on, isn't she?" A shadow of defeat passed over her face.

Janet smiled inwardly about that. It was so easy to get Billie down. "She might not be. It could be an unfortunate name, that's all. Where's he based?"

"On Moon's estate. He's got an office above the greengrocer in Waverly Street."

"Right, I'll go there after I've left here, all right?"

"What about work?"

"I'm not due in until two. It's only an hour for me to get home, and if I'm quick through the checks when I leave, I'll make it to my office in time."

"You're such a good friend. Go now, then." Billie stood. "I'll phone you later, about seven."

"Okay." Janet rose and made a pained face that said: *I really want to cuddle you*. She didn't, but it was only right she said and did all the expected things. "Take care."

Billie nodded. "I will, unless I hear bad news from you."

Pleased Billie still felt taking her own life was an option, Janet walked out, went through all the usual palaver to leave the prison, and got in her car.

On the journey back to London, her satnav instructed to take her to Waverly Street, she cursed Freda and her scabby scar.

"Interfering cow, isn't she."

"Look, leave me alone to think for a second, will you?"

She glanced at her face in the rearview and jumped at the sight of herself in disguise. She'd forgotten for a moment that she had her old appearance, the person Billie would recognise, the one the prison officers knew as a regular, and it still matched her passport photo which she had to bring with her every time. If she swanned in as her new self, Billie would have to look two or three times before she twigged who Janet was.

Now, should she visit this Randy Baker as the old or the new?

"The old."

"Why?"

"Because he might report back to Billie that you went to see him. He could mention what you look like with longer hair and no glasses, then she'd know you've been going to see her in disguise. She might want to know why. We don't need her asking questions, do we."

Janet should have thought of that herself. And if she paid him a second visit to…do what she felt needed to be done, killing him so he couldn't help Billie, it was best she had the glasses and wig on because of witnesses. Then again, she wouldn't need to do anything herself. She'd used Billie to do her dirty work last time so she wasn't involved, and she could use the twins this time, although she'd need to think of a valid excuse as to why she needed them to take this Randy fella out.

George would believe whatever she told them, she was sure of it, and whether Randy lied or not while strapped to the warehouse chair or chained to the spiked wall rack, they'd think he was trying to lie his way out of the shit when he told them he had no idea what he was supposed to have done to upset Janet, especially if she was there and he saw her without the disguise on. He'd genuinely have no clue who she was.

She smiled all the way to London, singing along to Radio 2 which cranked out songs from those heady days when she'd been in Sean's life. This would all work out, and with Randy dead, Billie would give up and use that sheet.

"You have reached your destination…"

Janet peered along the street, spotting a parking space, and slotted her car behind a red MG. She got out, paid for a ticket, and stuck it on the inside of her windscreen. She spied the greengrocer a few shops along and walked that way. A white wooden door next to the fruit and veg display had a sign above it: RANDOLPH BAKER, PRIVATE INVESTIGATOR. So his name *wasn't* a wind-up, then. Janet pushed the handle down and stepped into a square entryway, cream walls, stairs straight ahead covered in beige ribbed carpet that reminded her of rope. She went up and, turning right on the landing, stared through an open doorway.

A dark-haired man sat behind a cheap white desk in a grey suit, navy tie, and yellow shirt. He glanced up at her through glasses much the same as she had on and smiled.

"How can I help?" He stood and held out a long-fingered hand.

Janet walked in and shook it; his skin was soft, like Sean's. "I'm here on behalf of Billie Haiden. Her friend, Freda—sorry, I don't know her surname—said you'd be able to help."

"Err, I haven't had any contact with a Freda, although I haven't opened the post yet." He gestured to a stack of letters beside his open laptop.

She didn't spot the familiar prison one amongst the others and relaxed. "Oh, right, it's just that I've come from the prison, that's where Billie and Freda are, and—"

"Ah, *that* Freda. Unfortunate business." He sat and balanced an ankle on his opposing knee.

"Is there a problem?" *Please say yes.*

"No, no, it's…" He cleared his throat. "Am I being retained by you or Freda? I'd like to make it clear I can't talk to you about anything unless you're employing me."

"No, it'll be Freda who contacts you. She said something about you being paid once Billie's been compensated for wrongful incarceration."

He winced. "One of *those* cases. Right. And that's not how I work. I need a retainer for expenses. I'll have to let Freda know that."

"Why would she give my friend hope by saying that, then?"

"Freda's…she's a neighbour of my mother's. Well, she was until she… She seems to think I'll do things like this for free because of them being close—and maybe I will if Mother harps on too much." He sighed.

Janet smiled to hide her infuriation. She *couldn't* have him poking around. "I understand. I don't want to sound off or anything, and I wouldn't want Billie to know I said this, but you'd be wasting your time anyway, because she *did* do it. She's guilty. She just won't admit to it."

"Hmm."

"It's a long story."

"Aren't they all."

Janet walked away and said over her shoulder, "Well, thanks for your time."

She left the building, two options floating in her mind. She could let this play out and risk Randy taking Billie's case on because his mother bugged him to do it, or she could have Randy sorted by the twins.

"I know which one I'd choose."

Janet got in her car. "Now why doesn't that surprise me?"

Chapter Nine

Ichabod's phone bleeped in reply to his message, and he swiped the screen, hoping he was instructed to do what he *wanted* to do. Mind you, George and Greg had a canny way of working, and they might think he was better off following Janet again. He accessed the message and smiled.

GG: GO AND SPEAK TO THE PI.

The twins had read his mind—or they were on the same wavelength. It was better to get information out of the PI than tail Janet to her office where she'd do her usual and chat to clients. He'd get no information out of that, whereas this way, he might get something the twins could use against her. While he didn't know what their plans were with her, other than catching her out at being dodgy, Ichabod could well imagine that they wouldn't be wasting all this time on her if it wasn't serious. Yes, there was a murder in her past, but so what?

They must really think she was in on it.

He checked the street to confirm she'd really gone then got out of the Saab, patted the inside pocket of his suit jacket to make sure the knife was there should he need it for extra persuasion, and walked up to the white door. He didn't give a fuck about anyone clocking him, and he assumed the twins would have squared it away with Moon that he was doing Cardigan business on his estate. Nobody appeared to take any notice of him, everyone minding their own business, nipping into shops or nagging at the kerbs.

He glanced up. No one stared down at him from the windows.

He opened the door. Inside the small hallway, he dropped the snib on the Yale lock to prevent anyone else coming in. If he had to produce his knife, it was best not to have anyone walking in on him using it. He noted a door marked PRIVATE and assumed it led into the shop next door; a quick tug on the handle to check if it was locked, and he was happy he wouldn't be disturbed.

He went upstairs, going quietly, watching through the banister rails as he got higher and higher. At the top, he turned right to face an office. No one was in there, so he flicked his gaze to another open door—a studio flat effort, a little kitchenette and the end of a double bed visible, so perhaps Baker lived here as well as worked. It was heaps better than Ichabod's place, so the PI must be making a fair few quid. A flush sounded behind the only closed door at the end of the landing to his right, and he waited for Mr Baker to exit what he assumed was a bathroom. *Hoped* it was Mr Baker and not some randomer.

A man with dark-brown hair and glasses stopped abruptly, a hand going to his chest. "Oh, you gave me quite the fright. I didn't hear anyone come in."

Feckin' posh bastard. Easy enough tae scare.

"Can I help you? Randolph Baker here." He held a hand out.

Ichabod eyed it to make sure it looked damp all over—he wasn't shaking the hand of someone who didn't clean it after taking a jimmy riddle.

"Did ye wash?" Ichabod asked.

Baker frowned. "Um, yes. Doesn't everyone?"

"No, they don't, the filthy feckers." He shook the proffered hand, glad when the scent of soap wafted up. "I'm here tae talk about the woman who just left."

Baker folded his lips over his teeth and inhaled through his nose. He parted his generous lips and let the breath out. "Oh. Right. A bit unusual. Shall we go into my office, then?"

Ichabod moved to one side so the man could pass. He didn't like having his back to anyone, and for all he knew, Baker could clonk him over the head. It was unlikely, but back in the day, he had trusted someone who'd done just that. Never again.

"Strange conversation with her," Baker said and strode down the landing at a brisk clip, arms swinging. "I wasn't quite sure what she actually wanted." He disappeared into the office. "She said she was here to discuss a friend, yet she left without discussing much about her. Granted, I said I couldn't if she wasn't retaining me, client confidentiality and all that, but still, all very odd." A pause. "Hello? Are you still there?"

Ichabod had remained where he was, toying with whether to get the knife out. He decided against it and got moving. He wandered into the office. "I am."

Baker stared at him funny. As if he was scared. "Take a seat, won't you?"

"I'd rather stand, so I would."

Baker did the same, likely so he didn't feel intimidated. "Right, err, this is all very awkward, because if I'm going to be taking on her friend's case, I don't feel comfortable chatting about that with you. If you came to me to do a job, you wouldn't want me gossiping about it to anyone, would you. I pride myself in keeping secrets from those who don't need to be in the know. Mainly husbands who're cheating on their wives, but that moment when said wife shows him all of my photos. Priceless."

"I'm not interested in ye preenin'. I don't care about her friend or the case, just the woman who was here. Short black hair. Glasses. Jeans. A pink fleece. Literally just left. Her name's Janet."

"Um…"

Ichabod's need to get the knife out burned through him. "What, exactly, did she want?"

Baker's cheeks coloured. "Look, I can see you're a testy sort—"

"Testy?"

"—and I don't want any trouble, so if you're the type who's here to warn me off helping the friend, consider it done."

"The type? Yes, I'm the type all right. Tell me what Janet wanted, or so help me God…" Ichabod slid his hand beneath one side of his jacket front.

"Okay, okay… Oh, good *Lord*! Do you have a gun?"

"A knife, and it's goin' in ye gut if ye don't tell me what I want tae know."

"Jesus Christ! I don't really know anything. Some woman in prison wants help. I assume she thinks she's innocent because wrongful incarceration was mentioned. However, that woman who was here—Janet, you said?—she told me not to waste my time because the one in prison is guilty."

"Some friend," Ichabod muttered.

"Exactly what I thought. I really can't offer any more insight other than I got the gist that she doesn't want me to help the friend. Which I won't."

"I don't get why she even came here. Explain that tae me, would ye?"

"She said a woman called Freda would be contacting me to help the friend. Freda is also in prison and happens to be one of my mother's neighbours—until she got put away for murder. I haven't had any correspondence from Freda, so naturally, when Janet turned up, I didn't know what she was talking about—and I don't want to if someone like you is here asking me questions."

"I don't like what ye're sayin'. Someone like me. What's that all about?"

"Well, you're a little frightening."

"Of course I feckin' am, I work for The Brothers."

"Oh, dear God. Please, I want nothing to do with this. If she comes back, I'll tell her that, but like I said, she *wants* me to have nothing to do with it."

"This isn't making sense."

"No, it jolly well isn't."

Ichabod nodded to himself. What was Janet playing at? "If she comes back, ye let me know immediately, got it?" He drew his hand from out of his jacket and fished a business card from his trouser pocket. He placed it on the desk. "If this Freda gets hold of ye, tell her tae feck off unless I say otherwise. I might be back if the twins tell me tae come, so keep ye nose clean, and everythin' will be all right."

Baker's head bobbed several times. "Okay, right. This really is unnecessary, being so angry with me. I don't know what's going on, I don't know what this friend has done, and I don't want to."

"She killed a kid. A little girl. Five years old. If ye want tae help someone like that, then there's somethin' wrong wid ye."

"I don't!"

"Make sure it stays that way."

Ichabod gave him his best arsehole glare then walked down the stairs and out onto the pavement, sure Baker had been telling the truth. Just a shame Janet wouldn't if he outright asked her what she was up to. But he wasn't allowed to do that unless given the green light, so he'd go and spy on her office until it was time to get changed into his usual clothes and visit her for his walk-in appointment.

In the meantime, he'd bring the twins up to date.

ICH: FELLA ME LAD HAS NO IDEA WHAT'S GOING ON OTHER THAN JANET DOESN'T WANT HIM TO HELP BILLIE. SHE TOLD HIM NOT TO BOTHER, THAT BILLIE IS GUILTY. NOW WHY WOULD SHE DO THAT TO A FRIEND?

GG: BECAUSE SHE WANTS BILLIE KEPT IN PRISON?

ICH: RIGHT. BAKER, THAT'S THE PI, HE'S GOING TO LET ME KNOW IF SHE TURNS UP AGAIN. AND HE'S GOING TO REFUSE TO WORK FOR SOME WOMAN CALLED FREDA WHO WANTS HIM TO HELP BILLIE.

GG: SO BILLIE'S TOLD JANET ABOUT IT THIS MORNING AT THE PRISON, AND JANET WENT STRAIGHT TO BAKER TO PUT HIM OFF. WHAT'S SHE FUCKING DOING?

ICH: MAYBE SHE'LL SLIP UP LATER WHEN I SEE HER.

GG: KEEP US INFORMED.

Ichabod made a pit stop in Greggs and bought two bacon rolls, a chicken slice, and a coffee. He sat in the Saab and filled his griping tummy, laughing when he glanced up at the windows and Baker spied on him. The man appeared to be shitting his kecks. Or was he monitoring Ichabod so he could inform Janet or Freda as to what he was doing? Ichabod had dealt with many a schemer in his time, and although he believed Baker had told the truth, the man could be a damn good liar.

He fired up the Saab and drove back to The Cardigan Estate. He parked down the road from Janet's office and got out, walking to where he could watch her window without being seen. Two people went in for their sessions then left.

He had to get home and change. It was time to give her a load of old blarney and see which way the wind blew. Like Greg, he felt Janet was a poisonous snake, and he couldn't wait to help chop off her fang-filled head.

Chapter Ten

*M*aggie hadn't been back since the baby had died—that Janet knew of. Years had passed, with her and Billie growing older together, still firm friends. Janet had seen Dad on occasion, mainly when she'd gone into the Sickle for a drink on purpose. He hadn't been able to tell her to leave, she was an adult, and she'd enjoyed taunting him with her presence. It had galled her that he hadn't approached her for a chat, *to say sorry for what he'd done. She'd hoped, with him losing his son, that he'd have appreciated still having one child alive, but no such luck. Instead, he'd glanced over at her anxiously, maybe worried she'd get that look about her, the one he'd told Mum shit him up.*

What was that look? Janet had made several faces in the mirror, trying to see how she'd present to others when Maggie had a rage on, but all she'd succeeded in doing was appearing angry or annoyed, nothing like she imagined a possessed person to be. She'd long since decided Dad had lied to Mum. He'd used Janet being a deranged child as an excuse to fuck off with Alice. She wished she'd asked him so many questions over time, but it was too late now, he was dead. She hoped he'd died regretting his actions.

He'd been round to their house back then, the day after the baby's death. The knock on the door had been so urgent, insistent, that she'd thought it was the police coming to arrest her. Mum had already coached Janet on what she had to say when PC Vahedi had come round to take an official statement, seeing as she'd been in the vicinity when the murder had taken place.

The door had knocked again. Mum had gone out into the hallway and put a finger to her lips, warning Janet to stay out of the way in the living room.

"Where is she?" Dad had shouted. "That fucking nutter's got some explaining to do."

"Keep your voice down. Irene might hear you."

"So what if she does?"

The door had shut.

"Because she'll get the graffiti gang on the case, and we'll be forced out of the street. Is that what you want, to add your ex-wife and child being homeless to the list of what you should feel guilty for?"

"Don't be fucking stupid. Where's Janet?"

"You're not speaking to her while you're in that state. You've sunk the contents of a brewery by the smell of you."

"She put a carrier bag in my son's mouth. Did you know it was a bag? She suffocated him."

"You're thick as mince if you think a child could do something like that."

"She's killed a bird and hurt that cat and dog."

"Lots of kids do things like that. It doesn't mean they kill people, too. Besides," Mum had said, "she was at the park with Billie, and a few other kids saw her, so this is one tree you shouldn't be barking up. The police have been round already, and they're satisfied with what was said, so if you're trying to get her into trouble or taken off me, it won't work."

"Alice always said Janet would move on to people next, that it starts with animals."

"You bloody told her about our daughter? You said you wouldn't."

"I had to speak to someone about her, and anyway, Alice kept asking questions as to why I didn't see Janet at the weekends, she thought it was off, so I went with the truth."

"So here you are, accusing Janet because Alice says it must have been her. Lovely. So if Alice told you it was me, would you believe that an' all?"

"Don't be ridiculous. You'd never hurt a child."

"Which is why I've stuck by ours, unlike you. Why the fuck are you really here? What, you want someone to blame because the police haven't found anybody yet, so you thought the easiest option was blaming a kid?"

"He was my son—"

"And she's your daughter! She's no less important than him. Listen, I'm sorry this happened, but maybe you should be looking closer to home about this."

"Are you saying Alice did it?"

"No, don't be daft, but her ex might have. People talk. He's been angry about her marrying you and having a baby—something she didn't want with him."

"The police have ruled him out."

Janet had crept closer to the gap by the living room door hinges and spied on them.

Mum had shaken her head. "Right, so yes, it must *be Janet then, mustn't it. What a load of crap. Get a grip."*

"Who else could it be?"

Mum had glared. "You do not *want to go there. Believe me, if you try to get our child in trouble, I will kill you. I've had enough of your threats about doctors and whatever, and coming here, saying it's her… Piss off."*

Dad had raised his hands to placate her, his eyes wide in shock. "Calm down, all right?"

"You're only saying that because you know I mean it. I will fight to the end for her, understand? Now, there's nothing else to discuss, unless you want to up the child support payments, so go away."

Janet shook the memory into nothingness. She didn't like thinking about the past because it brought home how, even now, despite him blaming her, she still wished Dad had come back. She'd always wished it, couldn't get it out of her mind. She knew, having done all of her therapy training, that the wants of children sometimes got stuck on repeat in the adult's head, that they believed a traumatic event could have been be fixed if only so-and-so had happened, and many created a similar scenario to fix it the second time around. Just like a few of her clients, she believed she'd be truly happy if the person who'd abandoned her, who'd said they didn't care about her anymore, proved they did love her after all.

Stupid, because he was dead now, as was her dream of his return.

She needed someone else to pin her hopes on, and Charlene had her eye on the bloke along the bar in the Sickle. It seemed he was on a work's do, all of them in suits, talking about going places now they'd bagged a big client.

"Strike while he's high on an adrenaline rush," *Charlene said.*

Billie turned from paying for their drinks. "Ah, I knew you'd spot him. He's just your type."

Janet laughed, although some would say it was a bit creepy that her 'type' looked like Dad. She understood what it meant, accepted it for what it was: she needed a father replacement, and although she didn't want any fella acting like a dad towards her, if he resembled him, that was okay.

She pulled out her mental diagnosis folder and skimmed the imaginary pages.

Fatherless Daughter Syndrome.

His absence had affected her, ensuring she made dysfunctional decisions with regards to men. None of her previous relationships had worked. None of the lookalikes she'd chosen had wanted to play chequers and Monopoly, highlights of her life with Dad that she was desperate to replicate. She ignored the bad side, where he'd said he didn't love her in that shop yard, because if she found someone like him, she could make *him love her. Studies showed that a fatherless girl dived headlong into relationships that swirled with destruction, a chaotic pairing, and often, danger, because the lack of love and care they should have received from a dad pushed women into seeking it elsewhere, and when it didn't come up to scratch, things imploded.*

Grateful she was in the know more than the average person and could spot the signs before things got too destructive, Janet always kept her mind in therapist mode with men so she could save herself more heartache. As soon as it became clear that a partner tried to control her—the same as Dad tried to control Mum regarding Janet's childhood behaviour—she cut them off. All very complex, all very obvious as to what she was doing, to her at least.

"What's my type?" Janet asked Billie, curious to know if her friend had spotted the real reason Janet chose men like that bloke over there.

"The quiet sort, the ones who don't get lairy and chuck beer down their necks. But you know what they say about the quiet ones, don't you."

"Yep, they're like my dad. They fuck off with someone else."

"Hmm." Billie nodded to the fella. "He's married. Got a wedding ring on."

"Why don't you try being Alice?" Charlene butted in. "See what it feels like to be the other woman."

That wasn't a bad idea, actually, one of Charlene's better suggestions. Maybe Janet would understand Dad's point of view that way. She might be able to come to terms with what he'd done if she knew how he'd felt, why he'd chosen the path he had. While she'd sided with Mum, that Dad should have loved his child no matter what, Janet was stable enough now, and always interested in the goings-on of the human mind, that she could poke into how a woman could entice a man away from their child.

The gossip had filtered through to her as she'd got older. Dad had been seeing Alice long before he'd left Mum. He'd let people think she'd kicked him out—

which she had in a way, she'd told him she'd never abandon Janet to the system, so if he couldn't hack that, then he should leave—when really, he'd been waiting for an excuse to run off with his lover. Conniving bastard. Alice was just as conniving, planting seeds in his head that his daughter was a loony and it was only a matter of time before she got worse.

It had hurt to find out Alice knew about Janet, the things she'd done. The secret hadn't been a secret anymore, between Mum and Janet and Dad if Alice was aware, and Mum had worried right up until Janet had hit sixteen that she'd be taken away from her, that Alice would follow through on her suspicions and phone the police or blab to all and sundry. If Irene had ever found out, she'd have been straight down social services.

There had been a discussion on how Janet could get help without actually getting it. She'd gone into the medical field at Mum's suggestion.

"Think about it," she'd said. "We've tried so hard to fix you, but Charlene's still here. What if you could get the expertise to fix yourself?"

There hadn't been the question of Janet taking herself off to the doctor, especially not after what had happened to Mr Nasonova in the end. The poor sod hadn't picked up one of his prescriptions after a stint in the mental health wing, which wasn't unusual, but this time the lack of medication had affected him worse than before. He'd stripped naked and wandered around town, telling everyone the world was going to end for dressed sinners, but if they took their clothes off, like Adam and Eve, God would save them. Someone had phoned the police, and he'd run. He'd made it to a high bridge and thrown himself off, landing on the dual carriageway beneath, his brains spilling out on the road.

"If that's what seeing a doctor does for you, gets you even crazier when you don't take your tablets, why the hell would you want to go?" Mum had wrung her hands. "Will you do it? Fix yourself?"

Janet had nodded. She'd gone to uni with Billie, then studied to become a therapist. It had taken years, but here she was, working in a practise and helping Billie and her mum through their recent trauma. Billie's father had died, and the pair of them had taken it badly, so Janet had stepped in to give them pointers on coping.

"Are you going to chat him up?" Billie asked.

"I'm not sure I want another relationship at the minute," Janet lied.

"Oh, go on. They can't all be arseholes. And besides, with him married, you don't have to have a massive commitment or anything."

"I thought you hated men who cheated on their other halves."

"I do, but if it means my friend gets what she wants, then I can overlook it."

That was the thing with Billie, she cared about Janet as if they were sisters, only wanting the best for her. They'd been through everything together, apart from Janet sharing the secret. Janet reckoned Billie was that devoted to her, if she told Billie to do a Mr Nasonova and jump off a bridge, she would.

Why hadn't Dad loved her like that?

"Fair enough," Janet said. "I'll go and try my luck now."

Janet's luck had all but won her the game, and she had him in the palm of her hand. Sean, he was called, although he hadn't told her his surname. That would come in time, then she could find out everything about him, the same as she had with her previous partners. Following him would help to get a proper feel for him. Charlene was good at that.

"So why, as a married man, are you letting me chat you up?" she asked, desperate to know the answer. She pretended she was Alice and Sean was Dad, imagining their first meeting had gone exactly this way. "Not that I think badly of you for it." I hate you for it, for what you did to me and Mum. "It's just I'm curious. People marry for love, so how can that so quickly be forgotten?"

"Life happens," he said. "If I'm honest, I didn't think I'd ever talk to another woman, not like this. I thought Whitney was the one, my soul mate, but shit stinks, and things go wrong."

"What's wrong?"

"Um, I've got a kid."

Even better. "Oh."

He pulled a face. "Is that a problem?"

"Err, no. So long as I don't have to be a mother at the weekends, change nappies, or play with her, we're fine." She laughed.

"She's not in nappies anymore, she's two, and there's no way you could play with her anyway as Whitney would find out."

"So what you're saying is you're up for a fling and nothing more."

He shrugged. "I hadn't even considered a fling until tonight, but I'll be upfront about it, I'm enjoying

142

the attention. I'll never leave Whitney, not while we have a child who needs us. Maybe when Emerald's sixteen I'll leave, or if Whitney kicks me out, but I'd go for custody. I promised to look after my girl, and I won't go back on that."

He wasn't like Dad, then. But maybe he'd said the same back in the day and Alice had managed to persuade him otherwise.

She smiled. "Nice name, Emerald."

"She's a good girl. Lovely little thing."

"It's interesting, because when I asked what was wrong in your relationship, you went straight to saying you had a kid. So the kid is the problem?"

"No, that's not what I meant. Not in the way you might think. The problems started after Emerald was born."

"Did you feel left out? Like Whitney cared more for your child than you? That's how it's supposed to be, you know. A mother would do anything for her baby. Or she should do anyway."

"I realise that, and I'm the same as a dad. Emerald is my life. No, the problem was, is, that Whitney suffers from post-natal depression, even after all this time, so she acts a bit...nutty every so often, and the rest of her day is spent moping about. This is why I can't leave. Emerald needs me to balance all that negativity out."

Charlene didn't like that. "So what's he saying, that because Whitney's got mental issues he doesn't love her anymore? He's just like Dad, the bastard."

In her head, Janet told her Sean was just like Mum, too, wanting to be there for the child no matter what, and be there for Whitney despite her problems. Sean was a good man, even if he was contemplating taking Janet to bed.

"Is that all that's wrong with your wife? She can get medication and counselling, she can be fixed, pretty much. I'm a therapist, by the way, so I know how it works."

"Oh right. She won't take tablets, so it's pointless suggesting it to her again, and it isn't just the depression or whatever. It's like I'm only there to pay the bills and take Emerald off her hands when I'm not at work. I've been pushed out of Whitney's life except for that. Her emotions, I mean. She doesn't share them, doesn't care what sort of day I've had. We haven't had sex since before Emerald was born."

"So being with me would solve that."

He laughed nervously. "If you don't mind being the other woman, yeah."

She didn't mind. That was the whole point of doing this. "It suits me. I don't have a lot of spare time to give to a proper relationship, so a few shags here and there, maybe a meal out every now and then, I could cope with that. Sounds like it's perfect for both of us."

Give it a few months, and she'd change the rules slightly, get him to care about her. Later down the line, she'd test the waters to see if he'd leave Emerald after all, see if she was important enough, loved enough, for him to do that.

It was such a simple thing to want, wasn't it? Love?

She glanced back at Billie who sat on some bloke's lap in the corner, regaling him and his mates with one of her stories. Neither Janet nor Billie minded the other one going off with a fella on their nights out. There was an unwritten rule, unless they specified no men allowed, that drinking in pub crawls meant they were on the prowl. Billie craved marriage and children, whereas Janet craved a man who was devoted to her and would never leave.

Strange then, that she'd chosen a man who'd stated he wasn't about to leave his wife and child for anyone, therefore, she'd never have him permanently in her life, telling her he'd never abandon her.

But that was all part of her experiment. She wanted to be the woman who'd stolen Dad's love away and kept it all to herself. Dad and Alice had still been together when he'd died, so it must have been true love.

Janet deserved that, and she'd do whatever it took to get it.

"We can either go to mine or get a hotel," she said. "Go Dutch on the cost."

"Blimey, you don't hang about, do you."

She stared into his eyes. "Why should I? I'm ambitious and always go for what I want. And what's the point of dancing around the issue? You want sex, I can provide it. You don't want a commitment, I don't want to give it. Casual sex with each other, that's what's on the table. Oh, and if you really need to talk things through about your situation, I can help you out there. My fees are usually two hundred an hour, but you can have my expertise for free."

"What, therapy?" He sipped his Bacardi and Coke.

She rolled her eyes. "Don't tell me you're one of those men who can't admit they need help."

"Nope, I'm wise enough to know talking about things would benefit my marriage. It's a shame Whitney's not prepared to do it. Honestly, it's all she can do to get through each day. I feel bad for her, I really do, but a part of me wishes she'd buck up and get on with things better."

"Depressed people can't just buck up," she said, trying not to snap.

"I know. That sounded nasty, and I didn't mean it that way. I just wish she'd take the tablets she's been offered. To want to be better. It's like Emerald isn't enough to try for, when she should be everything to try for."

Anger boiled inside her at that. Dad clearly hadn't felt that way. He hadn't wanted Janet to be the main reason Mum got up every day. What the fuck had been wrong with him? Yes, Maggie had done things, must have inhabited Janet in a way that scared Dad, but he should have wanted to help, not run away with Alice and start a new, perfect family.

"Well, talking to me about it will help you understand Whitney," Janet said. She narrowed her eyes at his frown. "What's the matter?"

"Just seems weird that the woman on the side is offering to help me fix my wife, that's all."

She shrugged. "What's weird to one person is perfectly acceptable to another. Take it or leave it."

"I'll take it," he said. "What's your address?"

She told him. "So your workmates don't ask questions, make out I'm one of Whitney's old friends and leave here fifteen minutes after me."

He nodded. "See you later, then."

She smiled. "See you later."

Chapter Eleven

George never thought he'd be poking into Janet's past like this. Why had he contacted DI Janine Sheldon and asked her to double-check Clarke's findings? Why hadn't he just left it alone? If he had, he'd be none the wiser, but now he had knowledge of Janet hiding a huge part of her life from him, he was a dog with a bone, wanting to get right to the marrow. She'd lied by omission, and since Ichabod's revelation that she didn't want Billie getting any help, the plot had just thickened so much the sodding soup spoon stood upright.

What kind of cow *was* Janet? Why didn't she want Baker offering his services, presumably to get Billie out of the nick? What did Janet gain by her friend remaining inside? Someone they knew who was a guard had just sent word, after speaking to a colleague in the prison where Billie was, that Janet had visited her monthly ever since she'd been there. So was she playing at being a friend, acting out a charade? What for? Did Billie know something, and Janet felt obligated to go and see her so Billie kept her mouth shut? Why did she go there if she believed Billie was guilty? George was fucked if he'd visit anyone who'd killed a kiddie.

All of those questions swirled around his head, and none of it made a bit of sense, which was why he'd opted to see the child's father, a Sean Dobson. The scant information Janine had passed on didn't really give much in the way of why Billie and Janet had been at the party — in the report, Janet had been listed as a work colleague and Billie was her plus-one. That didn't make sense either. If Billie didn't know the family, why the hell had she killed their child?

"This is going to be upsetting," Greg said from the passenger seat of their BMW.

They headed to the other side of Cardigan where Sean worked.

"Yep."

"He might not want to talk about it," Greg warned.

"He hasn't got much choice, bruv."

Greg tutted. "Don't come down too heavy on him. It's not like he's done anything wrong."

"But I want answers."

"So do I, but being bolshy with a still-grieving father won't help matters."

The rest of the journey was made in silence, George berating himself for not seeing through Janet. She was good at subterfuge, he'd give her that much. She'd well and truly reeled him in. If she hadn't pulled that stunt by mentioning Dissociative Identity Disorder, the one she thought he had, he'd probably still be with her. What a div he'd been, letting her into his heart. All right, she'd only occupied a small part, nowhere near enough for marriage or whatever, but he'd actually believed it *would* go that far eventually.

He wondered, then, whether that gimp ex-boyfriend of hers who'd conned money out of her had really conned it. Philip John Farnsworth-Smythe. What if she'd *paid* him to keep quiet about something to do with that murder, he wasn't an ex at all, and that was why she'd been keen to sweep the supposed theft under the carpet?

What if they'd murdered an innocent man, thinking he'd swindled Janet when he hadn't? George had interrogated him at the warehouse, and Philip had admitted he'd scammed four other women—but what if he'd just said that because he'd known George would kill him anyway, no matter what he said? He and Greg had strung Philip up on the rack in the warehouse, and George had sawn the bloke up while he'd still been alive. Before all that, Janet had confessed the part of her past involving Philip, so had she been waiting to reveal an even worse scenario with the kid murder, then they'd split up and she hadn't had the chance?

He remembered what she'd said about Philip.

"...It's gone, he's in the past. He scammed me of money—and let's be honest, I was stupid to fall for it. He was nice enough in other ways. And why are you so angry about it on my behalf anyway?"

"Because I fucking care about you, that's why."

"More than you'd like, I'd wager."

He grimaced. Yes, he'd cared about her more than he'd liked. Christ, he'd been such a fool. All along, she'd kept something big from him, something he ought to have been told so he knew what he was walking into with her. She *knew* he had to be in on stuff so he could watch their backs in case surprises from the past reared their ugly heads. And call him suspicious, but *none* of this sat right. All this crap with Baker and Billie and some bint called Freda was doing his head in.

What the fuck's *going on?*

He swerved into the parking area outside a block of glass-fronted offices that appeared to house several businesses, a large, free-standing sign nearby with names of the various trades on offer. He yanked the handbrake up, jabbed his finger on the seat belt release button, and shot out of the car, *so* ready to turn into Ruffian and kill a motherfucker.

Greg joined him by the automatic doors. "What the chuff's flown up your arse and nested there?"

"Her. Lying. And that fucking Farnsworth-Smythe bloke."

Greg closed his eyes and massaged his brow. "Shit."

"Exactly."

"Do you think she told you bollocks about him, then?"

"Who knows." George gritted his teeth. "And we'll never know from him because he's sodding dead."

"Keep your voice down. Jesus." Greg looked around at a group of suits approaching the building.

George waited until they'd entered. "I want to bring Janet in, torture the truth out of her."

"Look, I get it, I do. I'm not her number one fan, but until we have more information, we let her get on with her life, right? As soon as we have proof, we take her to the warehouse. Can we just clear up why we're gunning for her so I've got it straight?"

"You know why."

"Not the crux of it, no. One, is it because she didn't fully open up to you and it's dented your ego? Two, is it because as a resident she should get treated like everyone else, and because she's linked to a kid killer, we need to make sure she wasn't involved on a more sinister level? Or three, all of it?"

"All of it, but I'll only admit this to you, and I won't talk about it again—I'm naffed off because she didn't think I was good enough to share it with. I thought I meant more to her than that."

"Right, climb down off your high horse and remind yourself, like I did with you yesterday at Debbie's, that *you* didn't tell *her* shit, and *she* might be hurt that *she* didn't mean enough to *you*, too."

"Why are you sticking up for her?"

"I'm not, I'm just pointing out that you're being a hypocrite. Again."

"I'm entitled to not tell her things. I'm one half of The Brothers. She knows damn well there's stuff I'd never share with her."

"About The Cardigan Estate, yeah, but not about you personally. Listen, you're in a right shitty mood, so let me do the initial talking with Dobson until you've calmed down."

George nodded. "Probably best."

Greg led the way into the building, breezing past a blonde receptionist who stood from her perch behind the desk and flapped a hand.

"Excuse me? *Excuse* me! You need to sign in here, please."

George spun round and glared at her. When Greg did the same and she clocked they were identical, realised who they were, she lowered to her chair and found her computer monitor interesting, cheeks flushing.

"Fucking jobsworth," George muttered.

"Pack it in, she's got rules to follow, it's not her fault." Greg stopped at an internal map beside the lift and prodded the UP button. "Level four. Bingham Associates. He's a financial advisor."

The lift arrived, and they stepped on.

George pressed the FOUR button, and the doors slid closed. His stomach lurched as the car ascended. They walked out onto a shiny floor that reflected everything around them—a sleek black reception desk, tall potted plants, a few comfy chairs, and a mosaic-tiled coffee table (*bloody ugly thing*). This receptionist was a redhead and favoured thick eyebrows that were clearly drawn on with some kind of stencil—they were too perfect to be natural.

"Do you have an appointment?" she asked.

"No," George barked.

Greg nudged him in the ribs. "Sorry about my brother's lack of politeness, he's having a bad day. We'd like to speak to Sean Dobson, please. It's a delicate matter, so I'd rather not say what it's about, but if you could tell him The Brothers are here…"

"Oh. *Oh.* Is he behind on the protection money, only I'm sure Martin was here the other day…"

"Nope, nothing like that," George said. "If you could just get him, that would be great." *And it'll stop me from wringing your fucking neck.*

She tottered off on high heels to the middle door of a set of three behind the desk. A quick tap, then she poked her head inside. She spoke too quietly for George to catch what she said, but with a quick turn in their direction, she beckoned them over. Greg entered first, and George took a deep breath and did the same. He had to remember this bloke had lost his little girl. It might have been a few years ago, but it would still be raw.

George closed the door and faced Sean. If mourning lived on a face and dictionaries had pictures as definitions instead of words, this man's image would be there beside grief and heartbreak. According to Janine he was forty-two but passed as ten years older. Completely grey hair. Skin ravaged by deep wrinkles. George swore, if Janet had something to do with his child dying, she'd fucking pay for it.

"Is something wrong?" Sean asked, already standing and shaking Greg's hand.

"Nothing to do with the business, it's more a personal matter," Greg said. "We're sorry to have to come here about it today, but as you'll find out, we want to right a wrong, and any information you can give us to do that, it might go some way to making you feel better. We don't think justice has been served with regards to your daughter."

Sean winced—it only lasted a second, but it was there. It *was* still raw.

"Um, right. Err, okay, so what do you want to know?" He seemed to fall into his chair, as if the mettle he filled his bones with so he could get through a day at work had deserted him. "Sorry, this…this is a shock, you being here about Emerald. I did ask around for a hitman, but no one was prepared to give me the name of one. As you can understand, I wanted Billie dead, I didn't want her living life when Emerald couldn't, and I was desperate for something more than the twenty years she got." He knuckled his eyes. "Sorry, would you like a drink? And please, take a seat."

George and Greg declined the drink and sat opposite Sean.

"It's only just come to our attention," Greg said, "otherwise we'd have done something about it sooner. We've got limited info from our copper about what happened. She has to be careful when she looks things up at work so could only have a quick read. We don't expect you to go through the whole thing as it's clearly still painful, but if you can answer questions, that would help us, all right?"

Sean nodded.

"Tell us about Janet."

Sean paled. "Oh God…"

"What's the matter?" George asked, his curiosity spiking.

Sean shook his head—it appeared to be a gesture to admonish himself. "I was such a bastard when it came to her."

Now George wondered whether Sean had treated her badly. "What do you mean?"

It came out a bit too growly, and Greg glared at him. George didn't like the obvious question he had to ask himself: Did he still care for her to have that kind of reaction?

Sean sighed. "This is something I've kept to myself for years. I'd appreciate it if my wife didn't know."

When the wife can't know, that means an affair.

Greg leaned back, acting casual. "Go on."

"I met Janet in a pub. I was out on a work do; we'd just secured a big client, it was the one that put us on the map, so to speak, so we were all buoyed up. Things at home were a bit...let's just say, after Emerald was born, my wife—that's Whitney—was too tired for anything and suffered from post-natal depression. It had been two years, no sex. Sorry, you don't want to hear that sort of thing."

"We want to know whatever you think is necessary to explain how you know Janet," Greg said.

"Right. So anyway, I felt pushed out, just the man who paid the bills. I didn't even *think* about how the birth and motherhood was affecting

Whitney. I was selfish, thinking only of myself, and when Janet gave me attention, I was flattered and, to be honest, relieved someone wanted me. It was obvious; she flirted a lot that first night. I told her I was married with a daughter, but she didn't seem bothered. She joked that being 'the other woman' suited her. She was busy, didn't have the energy to devote to anything serious at the time. Of course, she probably thought I was spinning her a line: *my wife doesn't understand me, we've grown apart, and I'm only saying this just so I can get in your knickers*. That wasn't it, though, things were seriously tense in my house. So we got together about four evenings a week. It was easy. Whitney didn't seem to notice I wasn't there. In fact, she was relieved I wasn't, she said so. As long as I bathed Emerald and put her to bed before I went out, my wife wasn't fussed. It meant less pressure for her while she got her head screwed on straight—her words—and I got from Janet what was missing in my marriage."

"How long were you seeing her for?" Greg asked.

"Three years, so longer than I thought it would go on. It was fine until a week before Emerald's fifth birthday party. Janet said she wanted more—for me to leave my wife and move in with her. I said no and reminded her that had never been on the cards and *she'd* been the one to say she didn't have time for a permanent thing. Even though I'd grown attached to Janet, I'd never leave my wife while Emerald still needed both parents there full-time. That little girl didn't have a clue anything was wrong between me and her mum, she was happy, so I didn't want to ruin that. Janet got annoyed. Said something strange that I'll never forget: *But I'm fixing you, and I need you to fix me.*"

"Did she explain what that meant?" George sat up straighter. "Was she giving you counselling or something?"

"Yes. She was easy to talk to about my home life. Some nights she went into full therapist mode."

She did that to me. We even joked about her doing it…

Greg leaned forward and rested his elbows on his knees. "So what happened then?"

Sean closed his eyes briefly and shuddered. "She went a bit weird. Sort of panicked, as if me saying I wouldn't leave my wife was a big thing to her, more than it should be. I can't explain it, but she was almost manic; things weren't going the way she'd planned, that sort of thing. She begged me to reconsider, even painted a picture of what it would be like living with her. I said no, and Janet lost it. She hit me. Punched me in the stomach. I got out of bed—we were in a hotel at the time—and told her we were over. She stared at me with this really weird look and said, 'You're going to really need me one day, and you'd better hope that when you come crawling back for me to fix your broken heart, that I'm willing to mend it.' I didn't know what the bloody hell she was on about, still don't."

The cogs churned in George's head. A week later, Sean *did* have a broken heart when his daughter was murdered. Was Janet that upset about him ending it that she'd... *Fuck me, would she really have organised something like that? But how did she get Billie to do it?* "Um, if you'd split, why did she go to your kid's birthday party? It's a bit fucking rude to ask your ex-lover to go."

"I didn't ask her, she turned up with Billie. We'd had a little gathering of Emerald's friends during the day and then continued for family into the evening with drinks, food, that sort of thing. Janet standing on my doorstep was the biggest shock I've ever had bar learning Emerald was dead. Oh fuck." He covered his face with his hands, breathed deeply, then lowered them. "Sorry. Sorry, it still gets to me, her dying."

"Take your time," George said, feeling sorry for the bloke. *Responsible* for him. He *had* to get to the bottom of this and make it right—or at least better. Even if Janet wasn't involved, they could organise for Billie to be dealt with inside. Someone would shiv her for a few quid, no questions asked, then they could let this poor bastard know that Billie had got what she deserved and there was proper justice for Emerald.

Sean stared into space as if seeing things in his mind. "Janet wasn't taking no for an answer, she was coming into that party or she'd tell my wife what had been going on."

"She said this, did she?"

"Yes."

"What was Billie's reaction?"

"She said something about being sorry for Janet's behaviour. I asked her to keep her voice down, Whitney or our family might hear. Janet said they'd definitely hear if she shouted into the house about it, so I let her in, and everything was fine. She didn't touch me suggestively, didn't even speak to me in a way that would get anyone suspicious, she just acted like she was a colleague of sorts—that's what I told Whitney and the police she was. I said I knew her through work, which I did, because she'd invested some money with one of our clients."

George's shit-o-meter filled to the top. "What was his name?"

"Philip Farnsworth-Smythe."

George blurted, "Did you know she was shagging him?"

Greg gave George such a filthy look, George apologised for his outburst and clamped his lips shut.

Sean blinked. "Um, what? She was sleeping with him?" Clearly hurt by that, he shook his head. "I've got no right to be upset—look what I was doing behind my wife's back—but Janet was seeing *Philip*?"

Greg nodded. "She told George that Philip was an ex and he'd scammed money out of her."

"Scammed? But I was there when the deal was done, I watched her sign the papers."

So she lied to me about that, too? Why? What was the point? Did she say she'd been scammed to see what

I'd do about it? See if I cared enough to sort him? What a fucking piece of work.

Sean went on, "Christ, is he a grifter, then? Isn't he legit?"

"So we've been told, he scammed other women, so you might not want to send business his way in future." George wasn't about to admit they'd killed him.

"I haven't seen or heard from him in ages." Sean scratched his head. "So she was seeing him while she was seeing me?"

"Seems so," George said.

"I didn't suspect a thing." Sean blew out a breath. "She must have met up with him on the nights we weren't together."

"It's likely," Greg muttered. "If you can handle it, tell us more about the party. Specifically what Billie and Janet were doing."

"Billie was acting oddly. I put it down to her being drunk—she was off her face after a couple of hours, dancing and whatnot. Janet was sober. I found out later, through the trial and whatever, that Billie had gone to the bathroom to 'let the seed sprout', whatever the hell that meant. Janet had supplied that information in her statement. Then…then my world basically went to shit."

He went on to explain more, about Billie coming back into the living room covered in blood, Janet semi-smiling at Sean, although he'd put that down to a nervous tic as she'd often smiled when unsettled. George could vouch for that, but he'd taken it as her being smug or supercilious at inappropriate moments, something he often did himself.

By the end of the tale, some things made more sense but others didn't. For starters, when they took Janet to the warehouse, George would be asking her what Billie had meant about that seed. It was weird, it didn't sound right, and he had a nasty feeling there was a damn sight more to this than met the eye.

Chapter Twelve

*N*o one could say Janet hadn't given it her all. *She'd continued the experiment with Sean for three years, and tonight, she was taking things to the next stage. She'd done exactly as she'd promised him so far, having sex and giving him therapy, and it was obvious the arrangement still suited him. She'd even go so far as to say he cared about her. His eyes always lit up when he saw her, and he was affectionate,*

touching her when he didn't need to, asking about her day and how she felt.

He was the perfect man material, and she wanted him all to herself now she'd seen all sides of him. She felt safe that he was the one for her, safe enough to move it along.

They'd just had sex in a hotel, something she suggested they do every now and then to spice things up. Him visiting her place was all well and good, but it had become too 'man meets secretly with the other woman' and she was past all that now. Yes, they went out for meals in the West End, and she paid for them to see shows, so it was kind of like they were dating, but she wanted the domesticity, the commitment, and she aimed to get it.

If she'd judged it right, now was the prime time to do it.

"How do you feel about us?" she asked, cuddling into his side so she could look up and see his expression.

He smiled. "I love what we have. Like we said from the start, this arrangement suits both of us."

"Arrangement sounds a bit...clinical now, doesn't it? Especially since we've got to know each other so well." Janet had only shown him the side of herself she wanted him to see—the caring, 'better option than the wife' woman, the one he should want to be with instead

of Whitney. *If he knew who she really was, someone who struggled not to hurt animals and people and spoke to an entity who lived inside her on a daily basis, he'd run a mile.*

"It's what we agreed on." He stiffened, closing his eyes as if he waited with dread for what she'd say next. Like he knew she was about to pop his balloon.

"I know, but things change, people get closer. New priorities spring up."

His eyes snapped open. "What are you saying, that you want more?"

"Don't you? You said last week you wished you'd met me first."

"I know, but…"

"But I'm fixing you, and I need you to fix me."

"I don't even know what that means, Janet. I can't be with you permanently. There's Emerald to think about."

Panic took over. She was losing him. Losing his interest. "She'll get over it. My dad left, and I've turned out all right." *I'm such a liar.* "Kids are resilient."

"She's five next week. Five. Too little for me to leave."

"But you can't stay stuck in that life forever, not when you have me and a better life to go to. Why can't

171

you grab happiness? Whitney isn't the one for you, I am, you know that. Please, can't you just think about it?" She sounded manic and asked Charlene to help her out, to take over, but her friend wasn't there.

He eased his arm from around her and sat up. Even moved away a couple of inches. Her therapist mind found the correct explanation: Body language indicates he's distancing himself subconsciously. Creating space between you shows he's emotionally detaching; to touch is to connect, but he's disconnecting.

He sniffed. "It sounds like me not leaving my family is news to you, but you knew damn well, right from the beginning, it wasn't an option."

She closed the gap between them so their arms brushed. We're connected again; it's okay, it's all right. *"But it's been three years. You don't stay with someone for that long if you don't care about them."*

He moved another inch, breaking contact. "I do care, more than I should, but I'm not going down that road. You're acting like this means more to you than it should. You were the one who said you didn't want ties, remember, that being the other woman suited you."

"I want to be the only *woman now."*

"No, not happening."

"Please, just imagine it, what it would be like living with me. You'd come home to a nice dinner instead of having to make it for yourself and Emerald—"

"Who would cook for my daughter, then? Whitney certainly wouldn't because she hasn't done it for years. How can I leave her with a woman who can't care for her properly?"

Did Dad think this way? Was that why he'd told Mum to sort a doctor? Had he cared for Janet after all, wanting the best for her?

"If he wanted the best, he'd have taken you to a doctor himself," *Charlene said.* "If he thought Mum wasn't capable of looking after your mental health, he should have done something about it."

Janet sighed. "With you gone, Whitney would be forced to care without you around to mop up after her all the time. You're enabling her. With me you'd have sex on tap, we wouldn't have to hide away anymore. Then there's holidays abroad, sun, beaches, cocktails, and we'd have so much fun. There'd be no stress because you wouldn't be living in a pressure cooker situation."

"But I would, because I'd take Emerald with me, and you don't want that, so things would be tense between us. I'd have to worry about a custody hearing. Putting Whitney through the embarrassment of

173

having her depression bandied about. She doesn't want anyone to know; she's ashamed. I can't put her through that. It's not her fault she feels this way, you taught me that. Get it into your head: I will never leave Emerald, and I won't abandon Whitney unless she asks me to."

Whitney didn't realise how lucky she was. Yes, her husband was playing away, but he'd go to the ends of the earth for her. The woman was squandering his devotion, his understanding, how he'd never do anything to highlight to the public what was wrong with her.

Jealousy reared up.

For a split second, Janet thought Maggie was back, but it was Charlene. She got up and straddled him, hitting him, slapping his face, punching him in the stomach. He didn't retaliate, just let her do it, showing her the measure of the man he was. He wouldn't strike a woman, even in self-defence, and he was fucking well wasted on Whitney, the bitch. That woman didn't deserve him, Janet did.

He bucked her off, and she fell onto her back, staring as he got up and grabbed his clothes, putting them on.

"I'm sorry," she said. "I didn't mean…"

"This is the end of the line, Janet. We're done."

Panic swept through her. "What?"

"You hit me, and I won't put up with that."

"Please, I'll never do it again. I got angry. I—"

"They all say they won't do it again. I'll never know if you won't because I'm not giving you the chance." He stuffed his shirttails in his suit trousers.

Pleading wasn't helping, so she'd go on the attack. "Look at you, all righteous, yet you've been fucking me behind your wife's back for years. If you cared for her as much as you make out, there's no way you'd do that."

"And I'm a bastard for it, but I'll make it up to her. Get her to take help. Tablets, whatever. She's sick, and what did I do? Thought with my cock, felt sorry for myself. Took the first piece of skirt who offered to open her legs for me. I was wrong. Wrong to do that and wrong about you."

The cajoling angle was needed again. "We can go back to how it was. I won't ask you to leave her again. Please…"

"No, we have to pack it in now. I don't condone violence in a relationship, and you showed me you can't be trusted. The first sign of not getting your own way, and you lost the fucking plot." He grabbed his keys and jammed them in his suit jacket pocket. "There's no coming back from this. I don't even want to see you again."

He stared at her, his face red with splotches from where she'd hit him, and she cursed Charlene for taking the reins. All those years, for what? Him to just walk out of here and not look back?

She glared. "You're going to really need me one day, and you'd better hope that when you come crawling back for me to fix your broken heart, that I'm willing to mend it."

He opened the door, shook his head at her, and left the room.

"If his daughter didn't exist, there wouldn't be a problem," Charlene said.

Janet inhaled through her nose. "It didn't work out too well with my dad's kid, did it, if that's what you're getting at."

"There's a big difference here, though."

"What's that?" Janet ground out.

"Dad loved Alice so would never have come back. Maggie was stupid to not have known that. Sean doesn't love Whitney anymore, not like that. He's only staying for the kid. If the brat's not there, what's he got left? Who will he turn to?"

Janet threw the quilt off her and stalked to the shower. "Well, it won't be me, will it. You've fucked that up by making me hit him."

"He'll forget all about that when he needs a bit of therapy from you, which he will. People who lose their children get into a hell of a state, we know that. The amount of clients you've had where mums and dads go psycho after they've buried their kids…"

"*You're bloody evil,*" Janet said.

"But I'm right. Leave it with me. I'll take care of it."

"I know you're having a time of it, what with splitting up with Sean, but I really need your help," Billie said in the doorway of Janet's office.

It was a pest when Billie turned up at work like this, wanting therapy on the spot. Janet sighed and motioned for her to come in and close the door.

"Not here," she said. "I get what it's like when you're desperate, but if my boss found out I was seeing you here and you weren't paying…"

"You should start up on your own. There wouldn't be a problem, then."

Janet had been thinking of that. She had a good track record with her clients, and some of them would likely come with her if she opened her own place, but there was the lease of a property to think about and the money to set it all up. She'd invested all of her savings with Philip. She could go to the bank with a solid business plan, she supposed, leave it to fate to decide her career path. If she got accepted, she'd move on. The NHS would refer people to her, so she wouldn't be starting from scratch, and she could advertise her services online.

"I'll look into it," she said, "but until then, stop turning up here."

"You finished at half past five anyway, and it's quarter to six now."

"I know, but we do sessions at yours or mine, never here." Janet closed her laptop, put the hard copy file away for her last patient, locked the filing cabinet, and picked up her handbag.

Waving to the receptionist and her boss, she followed Billie out of the building. Billie must have walked here, because she waited by the passenger side of Janet's car. Janet unlocked the doors and got in, swinging her handbag into the back, seeing as Billie's arse now filled the space next to her.

Janet put her seat belt on and revved the engine. "So what triggered you today?"

"I went to see Mum."

Janet drove off towards home. "You know it's not a good idea to go and see her on the anniversary."

"I know, but if I didn't, it would look bad. How can I let her sit by herself on a day like today?"

"Um, because she asked you to? It doesn't matter what other people think if she's requested for you to stay away. I know you don't mean to, but you're messing with her recovery and all the sessions I've done with her. I'm trying to help the pair of you after losing your dad, and as far as I can see, she's doing her bit, but you keep derailing her."

"I can't seem to stop myself. I need her on the day he died. She prefers to be alone, but what about me?"

"That's a really selfish approach, Billie."

"I know, but—"

Charlene gave Janet a sharp nudge. Now was a good time to get Charlene's plan in motion. "I can make you stop doing that if you want me to."

"How?"

"Hypnotherapy."

Billie stared out of the side window. "I'm not sure about that. It's all a too weird, messing with my mind like that."

"I suppose some could think it was, but all I'd be doing is putting a suggestion in your head, like every time you get overwhelmed with grief, it doesn't flare up like some monster. Instead, you'll switch gears and think of the good times, smile, celebrate the fact your dad was alive instead of being upset he's dead and how that affects you."

Billie ferreted in her bag for a Polo mint. "How does it work?"

"We go to your safe space, then beyond it."

"What, beyond the dune?"

"Yes, to a beach hut."

"Right... So what difference does the location make? You could hypnotise me at the dune just as well as beyond it."

"I could, yes, but it's best done in stages, so each part of going to the safe place has levels. Look, you know this, I explained."

"Remind me so I'm clear."

For fuck's sake. "When you first close your eyes and go down the steps, that's stage one. Stage two: you walking on the beach, me sorting your breathing out, you focusing on the scenery so it erases all the day-to-day worries in your head. Stage three: we're at the dune, where the meditative state means you're more receptive to listen to me, and yourself, about your needs and how to cope with grief. Stage four: the beach hut, where I take you a little deeper. You may not recall being there after a certain point, like that app I told you to use that helps you get to sleep. It's ten minutes of someone talking to you, yet you've said you only hear the first minute or so. It'd be like that."

"So I might not know what you're saying to me."

"No, but your subconscious will have heard it." Janet laughed. "Don't worry, I'm not going to tell you to become a thief or something and go and rob Mr Balakrishnan. Jesus. We're not allowed to use our skills for things like that. One, it's unethical and I could lose my licence if I got found out, and two, I'd never do anything to you that could put you in danger. If you're unsure, look the process up on Google, then come back to me if you want to do it."

"So you could tell me I won't ever cry about my dad again, just be happy that he lived?"

"Yes."

"What about Mum, can you do that for her?"

"If she wants me to."

"Fine, I'll do it. I can't keep going on like this. I've cried buckets today, remembering him dying, his funeral, everything. It fucking kills me."

"Then we'll make it go away, okay?" Janet turned into her street. "Do you want to stay for dinner?" She parked up and glanced at Billie.

"Please."

"Thought so. Come on. Let's get you fixed."

181

At the beach hut, Billie lying on the sofa in the living room with her eyes closed, Janet droned on, wanting her friend to be far enough under that she wouldn't remember what she said. She did a few tests to see if Billie was sufficiently in a deep state of meditation, then took a long breath. She did as promised, suggesting to Billie that grief wasn't to be a chore but a celebration of life, then moved on to her real purpose. Charlene's real purpose.

"When I put my hand on your knee, give you a knife, and say, 'Do you need to go to the bathroom?', you must let the seed sprout. The seed is as follows: You will go upstairs and kill whoever is in the bathroom. If there is no one in the bathroom, or there isn't a bathroom available, you will kill the person who has either upset you or upset me."

She waited for Billie to open her eyes and protest, to say there was no way she'd kill anyone, but she remained asleep.

"The person who has upset me is Emerald, Sean's little girl."

Janet smiled. If this worked, she'd maybe get what she wanted.

If it didn't, well, there were always other fish in the sea.

Chapter Thirteen

Janet was running behind. One of her regular clients had broken down during her session and needed more time to compose herself prior to leaving, which meant Ichabod walked into her office half an hour after his scheduled appointment. It annoyed her when things didn't run smoothly, and she had to tamp down her irritation so it didn't filter though to Ichabod. As he worked for the twins, she didn't want him running back to them saying she wasn't competent at her job.

"I'm so sorry," she said and placed his coffee on the table.

"Not tae worry. I saw she was upset when she left. Sounds like she had a lot of unpacking tae do. Emotionally, I mean." He sat in the chair and got comfy. "Does that mean I only get half an hour?"

"No, of course not. It isn't your fault it ran over. Aster will let the others know we're thirty minutes behind. I'll just have to work later, that's all—and no, I don't mind." She did, she wanted to go home and properly formulate a plan to get George back instead of thinking about it in wispy snippets. She sat opposite the Irishman and settled back to hear more about Kallie—or whatever other nuggets of info she could perhaps use to her advantage later. "So how have you been since yesterday?"

"I've got another problem on me mind now."

"Oh, do you want to talk about it?"

"Of course I feckin' do. I wouldn't be here otherwise."

"Sorry, that was a silly thing for me to say." *God, he's moody.*

She made a mental note to watch him for signs of flipping. Maybe he had a Maggie inside him, and if she was lucky enough, that person would show itself and she could study his expressions, his eyes, to give her an indication of what Dad had seen when Maggie had paid Janet a visit. She'd watched George teeter on the verge of showing her, but he'd always reined himself in. His self-control astounded her. She only wished she'd been there on the occasions when the red mist had come down. Greg didn't know how lucky he was to witness such a momentous thing.

"Okay, tell me about your problem." She smiled and crossed her legs.

Ichabod fidgeted. "I've got a conscience, ye know. Some things don't sit right wid me. It's like I've got ants under me skin."

"Many patients get that. You're not alone."

"I've been given a job. There's this fella I've got tae sort." He paused. "Do ye have tae tell the police if ye know about things beforehand?"

"It depends whether this is a job for the twins or not."

"Oh yeah, it's for them all right."

"Then I'll pretend you haven't told me anything." As she still wanted to win George

187

back, she'd keep her mouth shut. The day he properly cast her aside, though, she'd consider dobbing him and his brother in. She'd get a lot of satisfaction from seeing those two go down.

"Ye're good at keepin' secrets, then?" Ichabod asked.

She smiled. "I have to be in my job. People confide in me. I would be doing them an injustice if I revealed whatever they said."

"Do ye keep secrets for other people? Not the ones who come for the therapy?"

"Um, I have been known to, yes." *Why did he ask that?*

"What about secrets on yerself? Have ye got a few of those?"

She smiled again to hide her unease. "Hasn't everyone?"

"I suppose so."

"Why the need to know?"

"Because if ye've got yer own secrets, ye'll be more understandin' as tae me havin' them."

"Okay…"

"Right, so when I tell ye there's this man and he killed a kid, ye'll get why I've been given the job. Five years old, she was."

Janet schooled her features. Five years old was a sore subject with her. "How *awful*. Why did he do that?"

"Fecked if I know, I just have tae sort him. Ye know how it is wid them twins. Ye take ye orders and do the work, no questions asked. But I'm strugglin' wid the whys and wherefores, ye know? I prefer tae know exactly what I'm walkin' into, so I can make me mind up on *how* he needs tae be sorted. A man who kills a kid must have a bloody good reason. We're not talkin' paedophile here, I know that much, so how come he did it?"

"I can't answer that. All I can do is help with your feelings on the matter."

"I should know what I'm dealing wid, then ye might know what tae advise. Hang on while I message The Brothers and get more information."

While he did that, Janet had a go at settling her nerves. The mention of a five-year-old had shredded them, and she'd had the urge to tell Ichabod she was feeling unwell and needed to reschedule. She'd battled that need, though, unwilling to let the memories affect her life. Sean was a distant memory now she had George to concentrate on—for a second time. She'd made a mistake with Sean by showing her hand, getting manic, and allowing him to finish with her; that's why, with George, she'd got in there first so there wasn't a repeat of the past, and she'd remained calm with him, unlike her ridiculous, pathetic, needy outburst with Sean in the hotel room. Now, she had to ensure there wasn't *another* repeat; her relationship with Sean had ended for good, whereas if she played her cards right, the one with George wouldn't.

Her mind became muddied with that horrible sludge that glooped in every so often, where her brain was overloaded and she couldn't think straight. With Billie allowing Freda to instigate contact with Randy Baker, and Janet still trying to come up with a reasonable excuse for the twins to kill Randy on her behalf so it pushed Billie to use the sheet, and now Ichabod dredging up visuals of Emerald in that bath, Janet panicked a little.

"Calm down, it'll be all right. Let me take over. I'll look after you."

"Okay," Ichabod said after several message chimes, "I've got a bit more tae go on. There was a love triangle. The man was havin' an affair wid the kid's mother. He asked her tae run away wid him, but she wouldn't leave the kid or her husband. Man got arsey and killed the kid in an act of revenge."

Janet was suspended in a silent void as she experienced what felt like all her blood draining into her legs. Lightheaded, she scrabbled for composure. "Oh, that doesn't sound good." It was too close to the truth for her liking.

"No, not good at all. The mother has gone tae The Brothers for help. The man's in prison, and I've got tae get tae him inside, which is probably why George and Greg aren't doin' it themselves. I did wonder. How the feck am I goin' tae do that?"

"I don't know…"

This had too many parallels for Janet; she didn't believe in coincidences. Had the twins found out about Emerald? Had they sent Ichabod to play with her? Fuck with her mind? She wouldn't put it past either of them.

"They're getting too close. I warned you not to trust George, didn't I, but you wouldn't listen. I said it was dangerous messing around with him."

"Fuck off," Janet muttered.

"What was that?" Ichabod asked.

Shit. "Just thinking out loud. You know, that if I was asked to kill someone in prison, I'd be telling the twins to fuck off. Of course, you can't do that, though, so… What are your plans, to visit him and then, what, kill him? You'll be watched. There are officers keeping an eye out."

"Been tae see someone in prison, have ye?"

She blinked at him. *Has he been following me?* "Pardon?"

"Only, ye seem tae know a lot about how it works," he said.

She laughed, hoping it didn't sound as unsteady to him as it did to her. She wasn't going to answer his query but deflect. "I shouldn't say this as it makes me complicit, but I'd hate for you to get caught, which you will if you go down the route you've just mentioned. Can't you suggest to the twins that they get someone already *in* prison to kill him? They must know men who'd be willing to do it. That seems the most sensible option to me."

"Ah, ye're right, so ye are. That saves me havin' tae do it. See, I knew talkin' tae ye would help."

"It seems logical to do it that way. Sending you in there, that's dangerous, and very unlike them to not think it through properly."

"It is."

She'd play devil's advocate, see how he reacted. "Unless there's a reason they're sending you into the lion's den."

"What, ye think they're wantin' me tae get caught killin' him?"

"You never know. They've done worse things."

"I don't think I like the sound of that. Naw, they wouldn't do that tae me. I've known them since way before they took over Cardigan, when I worked for Ron and they were just teenagers." He seemed to mull her suggestion over for a few seconds then dismiss it. "What do ye think about this love triangle business, then?"

Bloody hell, I thought I'd steered his mind elsewhere. "It sounds like the man got desperate. Love makes us do silly things. Or what we *think* is love anyway."

"A kid being killed is more than a silly thing. It's the worst of the worst. Anyone involved in that shit needs stringin' up if ye ask me."

Ordinarily, she'd agree, but she'd been out of her mind with jealousy back then, desperate, and had thought with Emerald out of the equation, Sean would have come running back to her for support. That he'd have needed her. She could have siphoned off his grief to make herself feel better, except it hadn't worked out that way. He'd stayed with Whitney, cutting Janet out as if what they'd done in bed had never occurred.

"Bastard."

"Yep, that's one word for him," Ichabod said.

That was the second time Janet had spoken out loud when she'd only meant to think it. She needed some space, time to get her mind in order, and having Ichabod here was exacerbating matters. Time was going slow, though, and she'd promised him the full hour.

"She was stabbed in the bath," Ichabod said. "The kid."

Now more than ever, she knew she was being fitted up. Why? The Brothers had got wind of her past, and they wanted to…what? Force her to go to them and confess? Confess what, though? As far as anyone knew, she'd been downstairs at the party, in full view of a lot of people while Emerald was having the life stabbed out of her. To the outside world, Janet was innocent. This setup, Ichabod being here, it couldn't just be so that Janet told George and Greg her friend had killed someone. Why would they even need to know that? What fucking business was it of theirs? Maybe they were angry she was still friends with a kid killer. That had to be it, didn't it? She could explain that away by saying Billie was on drugs at the time and didn't know what she was doing. Surely they wouldn't look down on her for supporting someone who'd been in a *fugue*.

Would they?

"More to the point, Janet, who told them? And if no one informed them off the bat, it means they went digging recently. Why would they do that?"

"That's bloody dreadful." She remembered the pictures of Emerald's body in the bath, the ones shown in court to a shocked and horrified jury who'd gasped and cried. She'd known then that Billie's fate had been sealed. There was no way those twelve people were going to let her off, whether she'd been slipped drugs or not.

"On her fifth birthday, no less," Ichabod went on. "At her party. Ye know, some people are just sick in the feckin' head, so they are. Absolute monsters."

Yes, they bloody well knew. The story was basically identical. This charade, though, was stupid. George knew he could come here and ask her himself. Why all this silly business? She was going to have to come clean, but in a casual way. Ichabod could then trot off and inform the twins, and all this would be put to bed.

"If it helps," she said, "I had a friend who did *exactly* the same thing." She registered his fake surprise. "I *know*, coincidences are so *weird*, aren't they? What you've described is uncannily accurate, so I'm wondering if the twins have spun you a yarn and are really referring to what happened to my friend. They could be using you for whatever reason. She wasn't involved in a love triangle, though, I was, but she *did* kill my lover's little girl, on her fifth birthday, at her party. In. The. Bath."

"What are the odds of that?" He picked at a hangnail but kept a steady eye on her. "Why the feck are they sendin' me tae tell ye about it? What's the point in that? And does that mean they'll be askin' me tae get ye tae kill your friend?"

"I don't know, but their minds work differently to yours and mine. Their reasons will become clear. It's unlikely you're going to tell them to bugger off if they ask you to do something for them, so there's no point in discussing that."

"Why did Billie kill the child?" he asked.

I didn't tell him her name... The fool has fucked up. "Billie?"

"That's her name, isn't it?"

"It is, but I never mentioned it."

"I'm sure ye did, otherwise I wouldn't have said it."

"I didn't, but not to worry, I realise you're only doing as you're told. I won't mention your slip-up to them. And I still have no idea why she did it. She claims she didn't, she went into some kind of mental state where her mind blanked it out, but of *course* she did it. She was covered in blood for a start. It was awful. She was drunk—or so I thought—but it turned out she was hyped up on LSD. That, mixed with the alcohol, flicked a switch. She's serving twenty years, but I suspect you already know this."

"Ye should tell The Brothers. She needs tae be taken out."

"Now you mention it, yes, she does." She sighed. "I never told them because it's painful, thinking about that little girl, and also the fact I loved her father—the breakup hurt me. I tend not to talk or think about it."

"Sorry tae hear that. Do ye want *me* tae tell them your side of it? Save ye gettin' upset?"

"Would you?" She turned her tear-filled eyes to him. "That's very kind."

"No problem." He stood and glanced at the wall clock. "It only took ye half an hour to fix me after all."

For a moment, hope blossomed, that she'd *actually* fixed him, but seeing his face, she realised it was just an expression—she'd fixed him *for now*, fixed his issue of having to tell her, in a roundabout way, that the twins knew her business. How weird that he was acting as if she hadn't cottoned on to what they were all up to. As if he was sticking to the hidden script, even though she'd basically read it now and knew how this was going to end.

"I hope George and Greg go with your suggestion," she said. "You know, about getting an inmate to deal with the killer."

"I'm sure they'll see the sense it in. I'll leave ye be. Ye look a wee bit upset."

"Oh no, I'll be fine."

She showed him out, relieved Aster had warned the next client to come later. No one sat in the waiting area. Ichabod loped out of the building, and Janet retreated to her office, closed the door, and leaned on it.

Anger burned, bright and searing. George must think she was stupid if he didn't realise she'd have twigged what was going on. What bugged her the most was that he'd sent the skinny Irishman to bullshit her instead of coming here to ask her about Emerald and Billie himself.

She had a thought, one that churned her guts.

Had Randy Baker phoned the twins after she'd left his office? Was he on their payroll? Or had he phoned his own leader, Moon, who'd then contacted the twins?

"But you never told Randy your name, so how would he know who you are?"

"I must have been followed by Ichabod," she whispered.

But why?

Chapter Fourteen

*J*anet and Billie stood on Sean's doorstep. It felt so
dangerous coming here, and it was, especially if
things went wrong, but the thrill of moving things
along in the experiment had Janet bouncing from foot
to foot. She wanted to laugh manically, but Billie
would think that was strange. How annoying to have
to keep her mania to herself. This was exciting, seeing
if Charlene was right and that despite Janet hitting

Sean, he'd come running to her for help when his precious child was found dead.

While they'd been getting ready earlier, Janet had questioned Charlene's tactics.

"Let me spell it out for you, then," *Charlene had said.* "Think about how abused kids still want to stay with their parents when the time comes for them to be taken away."

"What's your point? Or are you trying to scare me with thoughts of the social for whatever warped reason? I'm not little anymore, it doesn't shit me up like it used to."

"I'm not trying to shit you up, no, more trying to remind you why Sean will seek you out. Children's parents, despite being horrible to them, are their anchor. It sounds mad that scared kids also get comfort from what they know—it's the same with abused partners. That's why it's so hard to run away because what they go through, even though it's nasty, it's familiar, and running into the unknown isn't."

"And?"

"You hit Sean, but you also gave him therapy, so you represent someone who can make him feel better. No one else knows what he's been going through but you. The lure of you giving him

202

comfort is bigger than staying away because you punched him. See?"

Janet smiled now. It made perfect sense.

"I don't get why you want to give the kid a present," Billie said. "What's the point of it? Oh God, you're not thinking of going inside, are you?"

"Of course I am. I just want to see Whitney for myself, see if he's been lying to me all this time. He said she's depressed, can't be arsed to do anything, like she's some kind of drip, but what if she isn't? What if he spun me that line so he could get in my knickers?"

"What does it matter if he did? You only wanted sex anyway."

"I know, but— Shh, someone's coming."

A silhouette filled the wavy-patterned glass in the front door, and Sean opened it. He stood there, smiling, in host mode, ready to welcome another guest. Then his mouth dropped open, and his cheeks flared red.

"What the hell are you doing here?" *he seethed under his breath.* "Fucking hell, Janet!"

That manic laughter asked to come out, but she told it to fuck off. Now wasn't the time. She held up a pink-wrapped gift. "You said Emerald was having a party, so here we are."

He looked to a doorway where children's music and chatter spilled out, then made eye contact with Janet.

203

He silently pleaded with her, and when that didn't work: "How am I going to explain where the present came from? Take it back."

"Say I'm a work colleague, I don't care." She smirked. "Unless people from your office are here. I remember you telling them that first night in the pub I was your wife's friend, so that could get a bit awkward."

"Janet…"

"Out of the way, then. Let us in."

He closed the door slightly. "Are you insane? How the fuck can I let you in after what we did?"

"It doesn't matter what we did, I want to go to the party, and anyway, you had no trouble living a double life before, lying to them all, so you can lie again now."

"No!"

She was done with being nice. Or Charlene was. She leant forward and said quietly, "I'm going to that party whether you like it or not, and if you don't move out of the fucking way, I'll tell Whitney everything."

Shocked wrenched at his features, and he caught flies. "Janet, this isn't funny."

"I'm not laughing." She turned to Billie. "Do you see me laughing?"

He appealed to Billie, eyes watering. "Tell her, will you? For fuck's sake, get her to see sense."

"I'm sorry," Billie said, a bit too loudly. She'd already had a glass of wine before they'd set off. "I didn't know she wanted to actually come in, just that she was bringing a present."

Sean glanced over his shoulder again, down the hallway and into the living room, then back at them. "Keep your voice down, will you? Whitney or our families might hear."

Janet gritted her teeth. "They'll fucking well hear if I shout about what we've been up to. That music's not that loud, someone will hear me. I'm being nice at the minute, not letting them listen to what I'm saying, but that can all change. Let me in, I'll be good, then later, we'll go."

By that, she meant we'll go, as in her and Sean. He wouldn't be able to stand staying in this house with all that blood in it.

He assessed her. "I don't trust you not to say anything. Not after what happened at the hotel. That came out of left field, so who's to say you won't do something outrageous again?"

"I won't drop you in it. I just want to know what I've been up against all this time, that's all. Call it mild curiosity to see who you've chosen over me."

"Why would you even want to do that?"

"For God's sake, stop stalling, or are you doing that because I'll see your dear wife is the life and soul of the party?"

"She's still not well."

"I'll be able to tell that when I watch her, won't I. See if you've been lying to me."

"I haven't. She's putting on a brave face, but I don't think she'll make it to the adult party later."

Janet cocked her head and wiggled the present.

He sighed and stepped back. "If you even think about opening your mouth..."

Taking it that he wanted her here really, that he'd missed her this week and needed her in his presence despite making out he didn't, Janet stepped inside and walked from the hallway into an open-plan area, the living room part filled with little girls and two boys dancing, and adults near the kitchen section at the other end. She smiled at the kids, put the present with the pile of others, and turned. Sean and Billie had come in, and he looked nervous as eff. Good, Janet had the upper hand here, and he'd do well to remember that.

"Would you like a drink?" he asked, his demeanour completely changing.

He was having to act, and it was an interesting study. She'd be able to watch him for a good few hours and see how he was with other people, see if he'd shown *her the genuine article or not. See if he was the right man for her like she thought he was.*

"Coke for me," she said.

"Wine," Billie mumbled, eyes darting about, her nerves showing.

Why she needed to be nervous, Janet didn't know. Billie wouldn't have a clue what she'd be doing later, and she'd have no recollection of doing it afterwards either. Charlene's plan to go with the drug-induced, diminished-responsibility excuse was genius, so Billie might only get a couple of years in a little mental health place, a small price to pay for Janet's happiness and all that counselling she'd given her and her mum for free, not to mention her helping them to pay for Billie's dad's funeral.

Sean, slapping on a bright smile, led them to the kitchen end. Curious people frowned or smiled, clearly wanting to know who Janet and Billie were. Janet scanned the faces of women around the same age as Sean. There were several, probably all the kids' mums hanging round for the drink and food, and it annoyed her that she was on the back foot and didn't know what Whitney looked like. When Charlene had spied on them, following them around, only Sean had taken Emerald out.

Sean went to the double-wide fridge in the expensive, shiny kitchen to get a can of Coke out and handed it to Janet.

"Thanks," she said, and to the onlookers, "I'm driving, so…"

"Ah," a middle-aged man said. "Same here."

Sean poured a large white wine for Billie who took it too eagerly and drank a third in one go. A blonde woman frowned at her as if Billie was beneath her. She was probably the sort who did yoga and power-walked her child to school in her active wear, ponytail swinging, telling anyone who would listen that the environment needed saving then promptly got into a gas-guzzling four-by-four and overcontributed to the carbon footprint on her way to Waitrose.

A skinny redhead in black leggings and top, wedged into a corner of the kitchen units, touched Sean's arm as he moved close to get a clean glass for the bottle of beer he held in his other hand. Janet glanced away but cocked an ear.

"Who are they?" Redhead asked; she sounded like she was only asking to make conversation, not that she really cared.

"I know the taller one through work. She invested with one of our clients. You know, Philip? He came here for dinner, remember?"

"So why's she here?"

"Oh, we got talking about Emerald's party, and she dropped by with a present."

"That's nice of her. Who's the other one?"

"Her friend."

Your daughter's killer.

"Are they staying, then?"

"I thought it rude not to offer them at least a drink."

"Right."

Sean wandered nearer to Janet and struck up a conversation with the middle-aged man. Janet smiled at Billie who widened her eyes in a 'get me out of here' way. Janet ignored her and watched the kids, Emerald standing out because of her carroty hair.

The child looked like a little brat, to be honest. She had spiteful features, as if she was used to getting her own way and was spoilt. If the house and Sean's car were anything to go by, he had plenty of money and probably overindulged the kid as a way to make up for her having a drippy mother.

Emerald snatched a toy off one of the boys and stamped on his foot.

"Nasty little cow," *Charlene said.* "But not for much longer."

Janet swung her gaze towards Billie, but in her place stood the redhead, a foot smaller than Janet and who would fall over if a breeze blew on her. She was so thin it was painful, her cheekbones too prominent, the freckles across them stark because of her overly white skin.

Janet smiled. "Lovely to meet you…?"

"Whitney."

"Oh, Sean's wife. Brilliant. He's told me so much about you."

Whitney appeared bored. "Has he?"

"Hmm."

"Thanks for bringing a present. You didn't have to." Monotone.

It seemed as if Sean had been telling the truth. Whitney wasn't interested in talking to Janet, she was just doing it to be polite in front of the others. The woman didn't want to be here at all, that much was obvious.

Janet was far superior to her. Prettier. More voluptuous. She had nothing to worry about. Whitney was no rival. "No, I didn't have to, but he's said a lot about Emerald, too, and I thought, why not? Don't worry, we won't be stepping on your toes for long."

Whitney waved absently. "Stay as long as you like. Sean's getting a Chinese later when the kids have gone home, so you're welcome to join in."

"Are you sure?"

"It's fine, honestly, although I'll likely take myself off to bed about seven. All this is…a lot." She grimaced at the noise coming from the other end, the children getting a tad squawky.

"Oh, the loud music?"

"Just…everything."

Janet touched her arm. "Are you okay?" She took her hand away. "Sorry, I'm a therapist, so it's second nature to pick up on when something isn't right."

"It's that obvious?"

"Probably only to me. If you ever need to talk…"

"No. No. I don't do that sort of thing."

"Stiff upper lip?"

"Something like that. Anyway, nice meeting you." Whitney drifted away to stand in the cabinet corner again.

"What a weirdo," Charlene muttered.

Janet sensed Sean staring at her and held back a grin. He'd be shitting himself by now, wondering what they'd talked about.

"Good. Let him stew."

Three hours later, Billie was three sheets to the wind, the adult party in full swing. The music played *low, which wasn't what Janet wanted, but she'd soon remedy that.*

Now was the time. Leaving a wine-drunk Billie swaying to the current song, Janet went to the little toilet beside the front door and took the small square of LSD blotter paper with a smiley face on it from her purse and returned to the party. She poked it into the icing on top of a mini cupcake and gave it to Billie.

"You need to soak up some of that alcohol."

"I'll wait for the Chinese to get here."

"No," Janet said, "eat something now. You're at that point where you're making a prat of yourself."

"Bloody hell." Billie took the cake and stuffed the whole thing in her mouth, chewing away.

Within the hour, the drug had worked its magic. Billie's pupils had dilated, and she sweated profusely. No longer interested in the Chinese's arrival, as she'd be experiencing a loss of appetite, she guzzled more wine, complaining of a dry mouth. Her hand shook slightly from tremors, and Janet took the glass away in case she dropped it.

"Are you okay?" she asked.

"My heart's going like the clappers," Billie said.

As everyone was busy filling plates with Chinese from the sideboard, Janet used her sleeve to cover the handle and took a knife from the block. She held it down by her side.

"Bath time, princess!" Sean said.

Emerald stuck her bottom lip out. Charlene wanted to punch her.

Sean gave her a stern stare. "You've been allowed to stay up late enough." He spun to find his wife. "Can you deal with it?"

Janet couldn't believe he'd asked Whitney to do the honours—Whitney, who supposedly did sod all for her child. Maybe he was grabbing the chance to force her to actually act like a mother for once, knowing she wouldn't say no in front of all these people.

Reluctantly, Whitney took Emerald's hand and, after saying goodnight, mother and daughter went upstairs.

"Let's go up the other end and sit down," Janet said.

"I want some Chinese, though," Billie moaned.

"Wait for everyone else to fill their plates first."

Billie nodded and weaved her way to the corner sofa, plonking herself down and slapping a hand to her chest. "This has actually been fun," she slurred. "Especially the clowns."

"Clowns?"

"Yeah, the ones who just left. It's like a fucking rave in here."

Janet glanced around the empty area, then up to the hungry people who stuffed their faces with rice and noodles. A normal suburban gathering. "A rave?"

"All those people, look, dancing. Jesus Christ, this is the best house party I've been to in ages."

While at the beach hut, as well as telling her what she had to do when given the order, Janet had told Billie she wouldn't have Hallucinogen Persisting Perception, so no flashbacks of the event afterwards. Janet couldn't afford for Billie to remember the murder, so once she'd killed Emerald and Janet touched her in a certain way and said a specific line to her, Billie's memory would go blank from just before she'd eaten the cupcake.

Due to the low music, Janet didn't have any trouble hearing when the bathwater turned off or Whitney instructing Emerald to sit still while she went in the bedroom to get a fresh towel and find some pyjamas from the washing pile.

Janet laid a hand on Billie's knee and passed her the knife. "Do you need to go to the bathroom?"

Billie muttered about a seed sprouting and staggered into the hallway then up the stairs.

Janet worked hard to contain her excitement.

Whitney would likely walk in on Billie murdering her child, and with any luck, Billie would turn the knife on her, too. Janet got up and went to the stereo, boosted the music up to hide any noise from the kid, and walked back down to the kitchen end. She took a plate off the stack and dished up some food, glancing at the others to check what they were doing. Eating, drinking, talking. Sean laughed at something a woman said—is he fucking her now?—and Janet used tongs to pick up two spring rolls to stop herself from going over there and slapping the bitch.

A shrill scream broke over the music, and it came from someone close by, the active wear woman who stared down to the living room area.

"Jesus Christ," Sean shouted and ran forward.

Janet turned. Sean must have gone upstairs. Another scream came from up there, a woman. Whitney? Billie stood in the doorway covered in blood, a knife held beside her. The people by the food burst into panicked chatter, and someone cut the music. Janet dumped her plate on the nearby dining table and rushed to her friend, feigning deep concern.

She gripped Billie's shoulders and shook her. "Oh my God, Billie, what have you done?" The coded sentence to prevent Billie from remembering.

Billie blinked in confusion and glanced down at the knife. "I don't...I don't know." She sank to the floor, dropping the blade, and stared at it.

Active Wear backed up to the kitchen, where everyone else stared in shock, their meals forgotten. Then footsteps thundered downstairs and Sean appeared, looking at Janet who smiled slightly at the grief written all over his face.

He'd need her now, to take away the pain.

Then he lunged for Billie, and all hell broke loose.

Chapter Fifteen

George, Greg, Moon, and Ichabod sat in the Taj, curries in front of them. Their corner booth hid them from prying eyes, not that George gave two fucks who saw them at six of an evening. They were regulars here, as well as getting takeaways delivered to the warehouse, and anyone who spotted them having a business meeting knew well enough to mind their own.

The restaurant was at the heart of their patch, the owners loyal. There wouldn't be any hassle.

"So she knows we know," George confirmed once Ichabod had finished relating what he'd learnt.

Ichabod nodded. "She's not stupid, I'll give her that much."

"No, she isn't, and that's why I wanted you to tell her the fake story to see when she twigged what we were feeding her. I wanted to know if she seemed guilty, whether something as big as this meant she couldn't hide her reaction."

"She didn't look disturbed at all." Ichabod speared a chunk of chicken covered in red tikka sauce. "I'd say she was innocent of any wrongdoin', going by her expressions. Of course, like I've already said, she then told me her side of things, as if we were just chattin', and when I suggested passin' it on tae ye for her, she acted as if I was the nicest thing since sliced bread—as if *I* was stupid and didn't know what she was doin'."

Moon chewed then swallowed his mouthful of tandoori chicken. "She's had years to perfect the way her mug reacts to news. Not only about this murder but to do with her work. She has to remain impartial, can't let her clients know her true feelings about what they've revealed to her. I mean, think about it, George. The shit you've told her in therapy, and I bet she didn't bat an eyelid. You wouldn't have had a clue what was going on inside her head."

"No, but when we were an item, she let her feelings show a bit more." George broke up a poppadom. "Let's think about what she said. She admitted to having it away with Sean and that Billie killed Emerald. What she's maintaining is she doesn't know why. I've spoken to Janine again. The defence's angle was that someone drugged Billie and she must have had an hallucination, perhaps saw Emerald as a demon or whatever, and killed her to save herself. Not an unlikely scenario when you think about how LSD affects people even without the alcohol on top."

"So what's your problem?" Moon asked. "Why are you poking into this?"

"One, she didn't tell us about it. We'd want to know if someone's all pally with a kid killer. If we'd known, there's no way I'd have gone to see her for counselling in the first place, and we certainly wouldn't have recommended her to other people, nor would I have suggested she worked for us. Nor would I have contemplated having a sodding relationship with her. To begin with, I was fucked off about having egg on my face, but now? After speaking to Sean? I want justice for that little girl."

"Emotions are complex bastards," Moon said, "which is why you've come up with another excuse to make you feel better about feeling personally aggrieved—justice. It's a cover story for you to save your blushes, plain and simple. I'm going with egg or your face. You can't hack that she didn't tell you everything. She either didn't care or trust you enough to do so. Yep, justice for the kid will be the cherry on the cake, but the basic issue is you don't like feeling as if you've been duped. I get it, as leaders, we expect to know everything, and when someone isn't an open book, we get fucked off. We don't like people taking liberties."

With anyone else apart from Greg, George would normally deny it, punch whoever dared suggest such a thing, but this was Moon, who had an uncanny knack of telling it how it was and being unapologetic about it. Plus he was now their good friend, someone they trusted, and although Ichabod sat there with his mouth open, clearly shocked someone had called George out and wasn't afraid of the repercussions, there was no point in denying it.

"She hurt me, lying by omission."

"Did you tell *her* everything?" Moon asked.

"Nope."

"Good man. You don't have to. She does."

George nodded. Moon understood the way it worked. Double standards may be at play, but that didn't matter. Janet had a duty to inform them of her past when she was in their inner circle. George didn't have to return that favour.

Moon chomped on some chicken, speaking with his mouth full. "So I've been called away from quality time with my bird because…?"

"There's a PI on your estate. A Randolph Baker, goes by Randy," Greg said. "Janet went to see him." He explained what had gone on. "He said Janet didn't *want* him to help Billie."

"Interesting." Moon nodded to himself. "Now I see why there's a problem. If her friend was jacked up on drugs and didn't mean to kill the girl, why does Janet want her to stay in the nick?"

George let out a sigh of relief that Moon saw things his way. "Exactly my point. Hurt feelings aside on my part, this is off."

"Yep. But much as I'm enjoying the catch-up and this free meal, I don't get what the fuck it's got to do with me," Moon said. "You've already got permission to dick about on my estate, providing it doesn't cause me any grief."

"We just wondered if you knew anything about Randy and that if he happened to go *missing*, he wasn't an integral part of your workforce."

"That could have been discussed on the phone. And I've never heard of him." Moon sipped his brandy.

"All right, then," George said, "I wanted your input, and talking over a meal is better than on the phone when it's a personal issue."

"Fair enough." Moon sighed. "Don't let me go home without buying a curry for Debbie. I like to keep her happy." He smiled. "If you find out Randy's a wrong un, do what you like to him, but I will say this. If it's like Ichabod said and this PI geezer doesn't seem to know jack shit, leave him alone. Sounds to me like he's been caught up in something just because his mum knows some lag bitch who's mates with Billie inside. Freda. Now *her*, I do remember because it hit my wallet, and I never forget when people lose me money. She went down for killing some old dear in a care home. It cost me a fortune as I felt obliged to give the dead woman's family enough money to bury her in style because one of my residents decided to commit murder. This is the shit people don't see, how their actions affect our bank balances."

"How our consciences get the better of us, you mean," George said.

"And that." Moon stared at Ichabod. "I'm taking it that because the twins have brought you along, you can be trusted to keep whatever comes out of my mouth to yourself."

"I'm not after any trouble," Ichabod said. "I just want tae earn a livin'."

"Don't we all, son." Moon got on with eating his grub.

"So what do we do now?" George asked Greg. "She knows we know. Do we confront her? Ask her why she kept it from us? Let her guff on about being upset about it, that it's too painful to go over it? We know she's going to choose that option because she told Ich the same."

Greg shook his head. "Nah, let her crap her knickers for a bit. She'll be on tenterhooks, waiting to see what happens next. I like the idea of her being scared. It might knock that

223

sanctimonious air out of her. If she's involved more than it seems, she's going to want to cover things up. She might panic, do something out of character—and we'll be waiting when she does."

George grunted. "She's not going to panic. She's too calculating. Still, watch her, Ich. I want to know what she acts like now she's aware we're onto her."

"Onto her for what?" Moon asked and wiped chicken grease off his chin with a napkin. "Are you're going down the route that she got Billie to kill the child? They'd have to be *best* mates for her to have agreed to stab a kid." He stared at the ceiling. "Ah, but what if Janet had something on Billie from before the murder? What if Billie felt she had no choice but to use that knife?"

"You're on the same page as me," George said, "because I can't for the life of me work out why Billie would agree to it otherwise, *knowing* she'd be caught and put in the nick for years. How much do you owe someone in order to do that?"

"It doesn't make sense, though," Ichabod said.

"What doesn't?" George frowned.

"If that was the scenario, Billie wouldn't be sayin' she's innocent. She'd go down for it, as agreed."

"Nah." Moon dipped a piece of naan bread in cucumber raita. "They could have used the LSD on purpose as a get-out clause but it went wrong. You know, woman goes off her nut due to drug-induced illusions. Except the jury didn't buy it."

"What I don't get is, if we're thinking along those lines, *why* did Janet want the kid killed?" George finished the last bit of his pilau rice. "We sent Ichabod to her office with the theory that the so-called man in our little story killed a kid in a fit of jealousy. It's an off-the-wall idea, I didn't think it would actually be true in Janet's case. We just needed to know her reaction to it, to see if we were wide of the mark or not."

Moon bunched his eyebrows. "But what if you've hit the nail on the head? *Is* she the type to go to that level to get what she wants? Did she love this Sean fella enough to want him all to herself, no baggage with the kid in tow every weekend?"

George thought about how she'd banged on and on about DID and reckoned he had most of the symptoms, plus that other thing she mentioned about people wanting to jump off bridges or throw themselves out of cars; it had a proper name, but he couldn't recall it. She didn't want to let it go, pushing and pushing him to accept he had no control over his Mad George side, that he needed babysitting, for fuck's sake, so he didn't get caught. He'd gone on to create Ruffian to prove to himself *he* was the one in control, which he was as that persona. He only ever lost the plot as Mad, sometimes entering the red rage (*been there and done that a fair few times*), but didn't everyone do that at least once in their lifetime?

"Jesus," he said. "I'd hate to think she stooped so low as to have a kid killed to get her own way. She must have really been obsessed with Sean to even go down that road. I mean, what are we talking here? Emerald was the only thing preventing him from leaving his wife for Janet so she had to be offed?"

"Or Janet's off her feckin' rocker," Ichabod muttered.

"What?" George pushed his plate away. "I think I'd know if she was."

"I don't want tae be rude, but would ye, though?" Ichabod spooned tikka onto the middle of his naan and made a sandwich of sorts. "And I'm not being funny by sayin' that, I'm not questioning yer skills. But sometimes, the most

226

fucked-up people are the ones who come across as the sanest."

Those words had a chill seeping up George's back. "Fuck. Did I miss something? Was I into her more than I thought and had rose-coloured specs on?"

"Nah," Moon said. "She's probably that good at hiding it. Think about it. She studies people with mental health issues. She knows how to behave to cover it up because a lot of her clients will have tried to do that with her. She's aware of what to look for. Fucking dangerous bird, if you ask me."

Better at it than I am with Ruffian? Regardless of whether Janet had issues of her own, surely, if she did, she wouldn't be able to practise therapy. *But what if no one knows?*

The possible truth slammed him in the gut.

What if she recognises all that shit in me because it's in her an' all?

"Fuck me sideways," he grumbled. "Now it's been brought up, we're going to have to look into it." He didn't want to believe it, though. To have it proved that he'd missed a vital flaw in Janet when Greg had often mentioned there was something about her he couldn't put his finger on was a bitter pill. That could mean George was losing his touch, and it riled him up. He thought about the posh doctor on their books. "Remington can help us out. Poke into her medical records."

"Best to get her checked out thoroughly before you make any rash moves," Moon said. "She's too prominent in your workforce for it to go unnoticed if she was sorted. People would ask questions and want to know where she was. You'd have to find a new therapist since you've offered her services to anyone who needs it."

"Easily done," Greg said. "She moved away, we replaced her, end of."

Moon swigged some brandy. "Anything you want me to do?"

"Maybe find everything you can on this Freda," Greg said, "seeing as she's one of your residents—or was, since she's now in the nick."

"Why?" George asked.

Greg tutted. "Fuck me, *think*! In case she's someone who can bring problems to our door."

Moon chuckled. "It'd be amusing to use that Randy fella for that. Employ the bloke Janet warned off. Poetic justice."

George nodded. "I'll send you a picture of her in disguise so you can remind Randy of who we're dealing with. And make sure he knows the consequences if he opens his mouth to his mother, Freda, Billie, or Janet."

Moon grunted. "What do you take me for, a fucking novice?"

"Just thinking out loud."

"I was gonna say…"

Ichabod swallowed the last of his naan sandwich. "So you want me tae carry on followin' her."

"Yeah." George sipped some Coke and fished in his suit pocket for an envelope. He held it out to the Irishman.

"You've already paid me a wedge," Ichabod said, hesitating in taking it. "And I don't need hush money tae keep me trap shut. I've never told a soul about yer business or what ye ask me tae do, apart from when you said I had tae wid Janet."

"I know. It's called fair wages. What you're doing is a lot of work. Our man, Will, can do the overnight stints while you have a kip—I'll let him know to relieve you at midnight. As far as I know, Janet doesn't leave her place in the evenings—

unless she's got herself another bloke to take her to those poncy West End shows already."

Another mug to control.

He clenched his jaw.

What the fuck have you been up to, Janet?

And why the hell didn't I notice?

Chapter Sixteen

At home, seven o'clock, Janet sat at her front window in her disguise and watched the street. No one appeared to be around, so she left her place and drove towards The Moon Estate. She'd been ruffled more than she liked by Ichabod's walk-in chat, annoyed beyond measure that George and Greg were playing games with her. Or specifically, Greg. She didn't believe

George would do this on his own. He'd had no reason to look into her after they'd split up, and he'd acted normally in his recent sessions.

Was Greg doing this behind his brother's back?

On one hand, that was plausible—Greg had always seemed slightly off with her, but she'd put it down to jealousy. On the other hand, Greg didn't tend to do things alone like George did, so he must have persuaded his twin to poke into her past with him for whatever reason. The fact that she didn't know why really got on her tits. Had Aster picked up on something and alerted them? What, though? Janet didn't keep anything in the office that Aster could find; nothing on the computer or laptop, no files, no secret diaries. The only thing she'd kept was a file she'd created on her personal laptop at home, containing all the news clippings about the murder and the trial, plus Billie's letters. She'd been the perfect employer to Aster so far, and there was no reason for her to have gone running to The Brothers about *anything*. Was it another client? Had they sent someone to spy all along, someone other than Ichabod, and Janet had slipped up without realising it?

Jesus, had Maggie taken over during a session?

As she navigated the streets, hoping Randy was still at his office, she thought through every interaction she'd had since she'd told George they were over. As far as she could tell, she hadn't fucked up. She'd been followed, though, that much was obvious. She was convinced the twins knew she'd been to see Randy.

She glanced in the rearview. It didn't seem as if anyone tailed her—no cars had peeled out of parking spaces in her street to go after her, and those people in vehicles behind her didn't seem suss.

"But they'd pick people who look innocent. A woman, perhaps."

"Well," she retorted, "if it's that tart right behind us, then she's brought her kids along for the ride. Not sensible, so therefore, it's a stupid suggestion."

Charlene went silent at that.

Twenty minutes later, Janet arrived in Waverly Street and slid her car into a bay outside the greengrocer's shop, her tyres rolling over, and popping, a stray orange. The lights blazed in the windows upstairs, so Randy was still at work. Exactly what she planned to do, she didn't know, she'd just had the urge to return here and speak to him, to get his assurance he wouldn't take on Billie's case.

This confused her. Hadn't she already decided to have Billie killed by The Brothers, to put an end to this once and for all?

"That was me, and you rejected my advice because it meant explaining things. You said you'd prefer her to use the sheet."

"But now Ichabod's likely gone off telling them my story, they'd believe me if I said I'd had an attack of the guilts for standing by Billie. They'd agree to kill her, then."

"Maybe they've already planned to do that. Otherwise, why send Ichabod to tell you he's got to murder a kid killer?"

Janet leant her head on the steering wheel. Charlene had been talking to her a lot lately. How much could Janet recall? How much had Charlene said that she hadn't kept abreast of? That was the trouble with allowing the voices in. They had a creepy way of infiltrating everything, doing things behind her back, and by the time she'd worked it out that they'd manipulated her, it was too late.

What if Charlene had convinced her to come here and kill Randy like she'd suggested before, only Janet couldn't recall agreeing to it?

"I need to get a fucking handle on shit," she muttered. "*I'm* in control, not you. You're the one who got me into this mess in the first place, saying about killing Emerald. I let you have free rein, and look what happened. Sean didn't come back to me. He pushed me away. Told me to never go near him again. Your advice is bollocks, so don't bother giving me more."

She pulled in a deep breath, waiting for the voice to retaliate, to cajole, but inside her head, silence was the order of the evening.

"Thank fuck for that."

She should drive away, go home, phone George and ask to meet him so she could explain her carefully constructed version of events. Strange how he hadn't got hold of her yet. Ichabod must have reported back to him by now. Hours had passed since she'd seen him. So what was George playing at? Or *was* it only Greg doing this?

The old feelings of being out of control returned, of losing her grip and not knowing which way to turn. She forced herself down the imaginary steps to the beach and sat on a dune, watching the sea shushing to and fro. Instant calm washed over her, and she sorted through her thoughts—*her* thoughts, not Charlene's.

Be logical over this. Tell George about Ichabod's visit. If he doesn't know, then he'll realise Greg's spying on me for whatever reason. He'll be hurt his brother is going behind his back. If George does *know, go with the story that you've been supporting Billie because there's no way she'd have killed Emerald if drugs weren't involved. Play at being a good friend, one who stands by a mate. A loyal person. George will like that. He prefers loyalty over anything else. I'll say I didn't tell them because it was too painful.*

She returned her mind to the car, expecting Charlene to pounce on her, but she didn't appear to want to say anything.

"I don't need to be here." She started the engine, ready to ease into the traffic, but movement in the corner of her eye had her pausing. She glanced to her right.

What the fuck's he *doing here?*

Moon stood on the pavement chugging on a cigar and closing the white door behind him. Alien hulked next to him, one of his big sidekicks. Why had Moon been to see Randy with a bully boy? It could just be a coincidence, and maybe Randy worked for Moon. Paranoia dug deep — Moon stared straight at her. She held her breath, expecting him to recognise her, then remembered she had a wig and glasses on. He walked off towards a posh car and got in the passenger side, Alien his driver.

Heart rate going so fast she had to concentrate on her breathing to steady it, Janet listened to the whispers in her head.

"You're going to have to go and see Randy now to find out what they wanted."

"I don't want to."

"There could be a conspiracy going on. They all know what you did, and the net's closing in."

"But no one knows about me giving Billie the LSD. How could anyone possibly guess what happened back then?"

"Some people can sniff out trouble. You know what George is like."

"Fuck. Shit."

Alien drove off, and Janet watched his rearview to see if he stared at her. He didn't. She shut the engine off again and sat for a while, thinking about phoning George now, explaining, but this was something better done face to face.

She could gauge his reactions, see the cogs working. Mind you, he had a perfect poker face, so even if he *was* in on this...whatever it was...he could convince her he wasn't.

"What do I do?" She realised her mistake as soon as the words left her mouth. It was an invite for Charlene to supply an answer. She closed her eyes tight, rushing to the dune again to centre herself, to stop the voice from filling her mind.

She didn't get there in time.

"Go and see Randy, if only to put your mind at rest as to why Moon was there. It can't hurt, can it?"

Janet checked the mirror for anyone watching her. People milled about getting last-minute bits in the late-opening shops. It all appeared so *normal*, just an average evening. And like she'd been told, it was only to put her mind at rest.

"Randy might not even tell me anything, though."

She got out of the car, pressed her key fob, and entered the building. Charlene nudged her to lower the Yale snib, and much as she wanted to resist, she did as she was told. It pissed her off, being controlled like this when she'd done so well in keeping the voices at bay until recently, and the main worry now was that she'd do something and not recollect it. What if Maggie made an appearance? The one who obliterated every part of her, replacing her thoughts and actions with her own? How many times had that happened already and she didn't know it? She'd explained it to George about his Mad side, needing him to see he suffered from the same, but he'd denied it had ever happened to him until she'd pointed out his red rages.

He'd admitted he'd had blank spots in the past while killing someone. That sometimes he raised a knife or hammer, and the next thing he knew, his victim was dead and blood had splashed all over Mad. During those times, he had Greg to fill in the empty spaces, to inform him of what he'd done, but Janet had always been worried, when George had left her after a night out, that he'd do something bad and get caught because his twin wasn't there to keep an eye on him.

What was it she'd said to him?

"People with DID aren't sure who they are. They have other identities, with their own names, voices, histories, and ways of behaving. Sometimes, the other entities take over, and the original person has no idea that one of the others has overtaken their lives until they bump into someone who recounts a meeting

they've had and the person with DID has no clue what they're on about. Or they get caught for a crime they swear they haven't committed, when they have, as one of their other persons."

A nasty chill swept through her. She could never be sure what someone had seen her do if she wasn't aware of even doing it. Shit, had it happened again already? Had she had an encounter with George and didn't know it? Had he remembered what she'd said and put two and two together? Did he suspect she suffered with DID and had got it into his head to prove it? Was *that* why they were toying with her?

"He can't know, he *mustn't* know," she whispered. "I can't let *anyone* know."

She climbed the stairs, nervous, so worried that a switch would flick when she saw Randy, and from then on, she'd have no recollection of what she did. That must be how Billie felt. She swore her mind had blacked the murder out. All she remembered was needing to use the bathroom. She'd been so confused in court when it had come out that she'd said, 'Let the seed sprout.' It was so obvious this was news to her when Janet had given that in evidence.

Janet knew damn well what it was, though, because she'd put those words into Billie's head.

She stopped on the landing and stared through to the office. She could see him, so she was in control. If she wasn't, she wouldn't even be aware of being here.

Randy glanced up and scowled. "Oh. *You*."

"Hello."

He rose and pointed. "You need to leave."

"I just…I just wanted to explain why I don't want you to take on Billie's case."

"I don't need to know. I won't be taking it on anyway."

"Moon was here…"

"I won't be discussing why. Get out. Unless you want me to phone him and *he* can escort you to your car."

So Moon had got to Randy who was now too frightened to do anything except what he'd been told. She understood how the leaders worked all too well. She'd had a ringside seat from listening to George. Randy would have to keep his mouth shut in order to live. What she didn't know was *why*.

"Did The Brothers send him? You could at least tell me that so I know what I'm up against."

"You're in a heap of shit, and that's all I'm prepared to say. Now kindly leave the premises."

"Thanks...thanks for the heads-up."

She stumbled down the stairs, her heart so heavy. She'd thought George cared for her, but somewhere along the line, his feelings had changed if he was spying on her or whatever the fuck was happening here.

"He might be waiting for you to trip up, then he'll pounce. Your next date with him could be at the warehouse."

"Shut up!"

Out on the street, she flung herself into her car, torn between crying or getting angry—getting even.

"You know which option I'd prefer."

"I can't kill a fucking Brother, and I know that's what you're suggesting."

Charlene's laugh burbled.

Janet fired up the engine, checking the rearview. The street appeared the same as before, although a few cars were missing, people having gone home. "I could take him to The Place of Stillness, plant a seed."

"At last, she's back to being on my level. It took you long enough."

Janet drove away, fighting with the devil of old, one she'd so successfully banished through hard work and sheer mental determination. But that didn't solve the other voice, the one she had no control over. As far as she knew, she hadn't succumbed to that for years. Some would say only medication could prevent the Maggie side of her from coming to the fore, but she was living proof that if every aspect of her life was free from stresses that triggered her, Maggie didn't appear.

She was lying to herself. Maggie could be living and breathing, choosing pockets of Janet's life to immerse herself in, and Janet would never know.

She made it home in forty minutes, the traffic holding her up. Parking, she shut the engine off and removed the wig and glasses, putting them in the carrier bag and stuffing in under the passenger seat. She scoped the street for anyone watching, noting a man in a silver Saab pulling up, glasses, a suit jacket, and a cap visible. He slid the car into a space outside the house opposite her place and reached across for something. What was it? A clipboard which he rested on the steering wheel, and he wrote on it, his face a picture of concentration.

He was probably here to give someone a quote on something.

"He looks a bit like that Ichabod fella."

Janet's stomach flipped. She peered closer.

It *was* him.

"Fucking little bastard," she seethed and got out of the car.

This had gone far enough. It had to stop, and the only way it would was if she contacted George.

"Watch him, you know how clever he is."

Janet didn't need to ask if that was Ichabod or George. It would be Mr Wilkes Charlene had referred to.

"I know," she mumbled and approached her front door. "I don't need to be taught how to suck eggs."

"But you do. Otherwise, you'd have known what he was up to long before he sent the Irishman your way."

Janet had no response to that. She let herself in and messaged George.

JANET: WE NEED TO TALK. MEET ME AT THE WATER WHEEL ON TICK-TOCK'S ESTATE, 9 P.M.

GEORGE: I'M BUSY.

JANET: TOO BUSY TO DISCUSS WHY ICHABOD'S SITTING OUTSIDE MY GAFF? YOU'VE BEEN RUMBLED.

GEORGE: I CAN SPARE HALF AN HOUR. GO THERE NOW. I'VE GOT SOMEWHERE ELSE TO BE AT 9.

JANET: EVERYTHING'S ALWAYS ON YOUR TERMS.

GEORGE: TOO FUCKING RIGHT. TAKE IT OR LEAVE IT. I'M NOT BENDING FOR YOU.

Janet took that as a bad sign. Him telling her that meant he wanted her to know he wasn't pleased with her, that she wasn't important to him anymore. Not bending was him relegating her to the status of a no-mark and she'd be treated accordingly.

Safe in the knowledge he couldn't possibly know how she'd manipulated Billie—unless Maggie had told him—she sent him another message.

JANET: I'LL BE THERE IN TWENTY.

Chapter Seventeen

*T*he aftermath of Sean discovering a screaming
Whitney in the bathroom and a dead Emerald had
created a scene out of a film. He'd gone for Billie,
punching her, kicking her, and had to be dragged off by
the middle-aged man. Active Wear screamed on and off
in the chaos, and Janet dragged Billie away from all the

accusing faces while they waited for the police and ambulance to arrive.

Sean stood in the hallway, staring through at Janet, a man possessed. "Don't you dare take her home." He jabbed a finger in the air at Billie. "She stabbed my little…my little… Fuck. Shit!"

He shot upstairs. Janet left Billie dumbstruck on the sofa and went to stand at the bottom of the stairs, telling the middle-aged man, "I'll wait for the police. Has someone phoned them?"

"Yes, me. Jesus Christ, this is a nightmare."

Janet nodded and glanced up. Whitney sat on the landing outside the bathroom. The bathroom door was open, and blood spatter created a grisly image across the sink, the mirror above it, and the white tiles beneath. Charlene wanted to go up and see the mess, see the scarlet bathwater, but Janet forced herself to stay put, her attention drawn to the married couple.

"Where's Emerald?" he asked Whitney.

His wife rocked, hugging her knees. "In…in the bath."

"What? I told you to get her out and do CPR. Fucking hell…" He dived into the bathroom, bent over where Janet assumed the bath was, and swung a limp and stab-covered child in his arms, pink water dripping off her.

The holes in her body no longer spewed blood, it leaked slowly, the one across her neck a fascinating gash. Sean placed her on the carpet beside her mother and got to work trying to bring her back to life.

The doorbell rang, and Janet snapped her focus that way. She hurried forward, putting on a suitable expression, and flung the door open. "Upstairs," she gasped out. "She's upstairs."

She moved back. Three uniformed officers swarmed in, one going upstairs, the other two into the living room. Janet went to close the door, but the sight of two suited detectives had her beckoning them over. She caught sight of blood on her hand from touching Billie and felt the need to explain.

"It's not me, the blood, it's off the...off my friend."

Grey Suit walked up the path and gave her a tight smile. "And you are?"

She gave him her name, breathless. "My friend, she...she went upstairs, and the next thing we knew, she came back down covered in blood."

Brown Suit approached and glanced up the stairs, muttering, "Jesus Christ..."

Janet stared the same way. Sean stood at the top, Emerald draped over his outstretched arms, the uniformed officer shaking his head.

"She won't breathe," Sean said. "She won't breathe..."

Janet snatched her attention away and jumped in surprise as Grey and Brown Suits had come in and now stood close.

"Ambulance has just turned up," Brown said.

"If you can go in there, Janet..." Grey led her into the living area.

Billie still sat where Janet had left her, but one uniform sat beside her, the other standing to block her exit if she chose to bolt. Billie stared mournfully at nothing. Grey herded Janet up the other end.

Amidst the commotion of the ambulance crew trying to help Emerald—"What's the fucking point?" Charlene grumbled—the officers talked to everyone, Billie eventually arrested and taken away. By the time a forensic team arrived, everyone had been ushered either into the back garden or were allowed to go home.

Janet stood on the patio, consoling a zombified Whitney, a job she hadn't intended on doing, but Active Wear and her friends had pissed off, and no one else seemed to want the responsibility.

"I never bonded with Emerald," Whitney whispered. "This is God's way of punishing me. I didn't care for her, so He took her away."

Janet hadn't taken Whitney for a God-botherer, but the parallel to her earlier years wasn't lost on her. Alice. The christening.

"Hopefully Whitney's really gone off at the deep end and there's no coming back for her," *Charlene muttered.*

"Don't torment yourself," Janet said, blocking out the voice. "Many women don't bond with their babies. If you want to come and see me for therapy, to talk it all through, just ask Sean for my details, okay?"

"Then make her go to the fucking beach hut."

At the point Emerald was taken away, Whitney spotting it through the patio doors as the crew carried the shrouded body past the front window, she snapped out of her strange limbo state and screamed. She fell to the patio, gripping her hair and kicking, convulsing, and someone called for her to be sedated.

"Blimey," *Charlene said.* "Talk about an overdramatic nutcase."

Janet ignored her.

It was weird being in the Sickle again where it had all begun. They said things went full circle, didn't they. This was her last-ditch attempt to get Sean back

251

in her clutches, but going by his stony expression, he wasn't interested. She'd lured him here on the pretence of getting their stories straight about how they knew one another.

"How's Whitney?" she asked once he'd bought a pint for himself and a Coke for her.

Progress. He hadn't left her to go without.

Grief had ravaged him, carving deep lines into his face, his eyes with a glassed-over look as if losing Emerald meant he permanently viewed the world through a watery lens. "Getting the help she should have got years ago."

"Good."

"I'm dealing with a lot of anger over that at the moment."

She touched his arm, pleased he didn't shake her hand off or flinch. "Do you need to talk?"

He moved his arm, seeming to twig what she'd done, what he'd allowed. "Not to you. I've got another therapist."

"Makes sense. Why are you angry with Whitney?"

He speared her with an evil stare. "Because if she'd been a normal mother from the start, I'd never have turned to you, and Emerald would still be here because your fucking..." He gritted his teeth and inhaled through his nostrils. "Your fucking friend wouldn't have been anywhere near our house."

"One of your friends or family gave Billie that LSD, so blaming her isn't going to solve anything."

"No one would have done that. She must have brought it with her, taken it herself."

"She's never done anything like it before. Completely out of character. None of it makes sense. Please believe me when I say I'm so sorry this happened. I wish I could turn the clock back for you, but I can't."

He studied her, clearly found her revolting, and downed his pint. "This was a mistake."

"What, coming here?" She shook her head. "It wasn't. Like I said on the phone, we need to get our stories straight. Unless you want Whitney knowing who I really am. I told the police we know each other from your work—I suspect you already know that—but what if they question us all again and find out we were involved in a different way? Can you handle your wife finding out?"

"No. You're right. Sorry, it's just... I can't stop thinking that you're to blame, that if you didn't chat me up..."

"It's natural to want to make yourself appear white as white, especially when the result is such a tragic death, but you flirted with me, remember, you wanted it, too."

"Yeah, well, maybe I need to grow a pair and accept it was my fault, but without Whitney knowing anything about it. I can't cope with how she'd react at the minute, not when Emerald…not when she's only been gone a few days. I can't hack people knowing I was…I was fucking about with you when my wife clearly needed help."

Of course he'd want to distance himself from any scorn coming his way if it came out that his ex-lover's friend had killed his little girl.

She had to play this slowly. Mourning couldn't be rushed, nor could manipulating him to see things her way at last. She'd give him another couple of months of her time, and if he didn't show signs of turning to her for comfort, she'd set her sights elsewhere. It hadn't been a completely wasted exercise, she'd learnt a lot, and with the next man, she'd dodge any pitfalls before they could create an issue.

"I still want to try, you know," she said, testing the waters. It was probably too soon to be suggesting such a thing, but she needed to see where his head was at so she could plan accordingly.

He gaped at her. "Have you seriously just said us two can be together? After this? After your friend…"

He slammed his empty glass down. "You're something else, you are. My kid's still in a fucking fridge after being cut up in a post-mortem, we can't bury her until all the evidence is analysed, and you expect me to think about shacking up with you? Fuck right off."

She'd put his outburst down to grief, but it shocked her a little how venomous he'd sounded. He was supposed to be grateful to her for offering him a way out, but it seemed he wasn't at that stage yet.

"You know where I am if you change your mind," she said and walked out.

Dear Janet,

I can't believe this is happening to me. I've been stuck in this fucking awful place for a week with women who've done some really nasty things, and they think I'm one of them. I am, there's no doubting I did it, that poor girl's mother saw me leaving the bathroom, but I didn't mean it. I'm not a _proper_ killer. No matter who I talk to other than Mum and my legal team, no one believes me. I suppose I wouldn't if I were them.

The thing they're not getting is, why would I kill a child I didn't even know? What would be the point?

I've got no prior instances of losing control, no worrying stuff in my medical history, have never taken drugs before, so…

My team said they're confident they can get me off on diminished responsibility, like you said. Somehow, I ingested LSD—we can only assume it was in the food or drink—and it sent me on a bad trip. There's something that sometimes happens to LSD users, you probably already know this, and I did, being a nurse, where you get flashbacks of what happened. We can only pray that happens to me so I can give the team some idea of what the hell went on.

They're assuming I hallucinated, obviously, and showed me this story about some man who killed his wife because he thought she was a monster—like, a real monster with scales and big teeth. He got off, the jury believed him, so all I can do is hope the same happens for me.

I can't stop thinking about Emerald. What happened in that bathroom? It's so frustrating not to remember. The blood spatter analyst has recreated the scene, and the team have passed on the findings. It looks like I stabbed her in the back to start off with, then she flopped onto her tummy, I spun her over to stab her belly, arms, and legs, then I finished off with the slice to the throat. The post-mortem report came though, by the way, which is why I know the order the stabs were in. She had seventeen wounds. That amount is classed as a rage attack, an emotional one, but I don't remember feeling angry. Far from it, I was happy before it happened, enjoying myself, even though I didn't want to go to the party at first.

They're sending me to a therapist. It's going to be weird speaking to someone else, but maybe they can help unlock the memories. Mind you, like I said to them, memories don't get you out of trouble, they're not proof of innocence. I don't think it's going to work. It's like they're locked away. The last thing I remember is eating a cupcake. I was feeling a bit pissed from all that wine, hot and sweaty, but I was fine.

Mum's coming for a visit next Wednesday. I'm so ashamed. How can I face her? What must people be thinking and saying? I bet Irene's had a few words to throw at her, you know what she's like. The whole street will pick on her, you watch. She doesn't deserve this. None of us do. Whoever gave me that drug is a fucking scumbag for not coming forward about it and should be in here instead of me. What was it, a joke that went wrong? Are they too scared to admit they were fucking about and it went tits up? What sort of person are they if they can let me be put in here when it wasn't my fault?

Anyway, I'd better go. I'm getting angry, and I've been advised to keep my spirits up. If you can get a visiting order, that would be brilliant. We can have a proper chat. I miss you. Wish we'd never gone to that party—but don't take that as me blaming you for persuading me to go. My brief says I should tell the police why we went, but I won't. I can't bring myself to hurt Sean's wife more than she already is. Can you imagine her finding out her husband was having an affair and his ex-lover's mate killed her daughter? It's too bloody awful for words.

I'll write again in a couple of days.

Love you,

Billie

xxx

On Tuesday, the day before Billie's mum, Kath, was due to visit her daughter, Janet sat with Kath, drinking coffee while the woman went to the dune. Kath was used to doing it now, and she needed The Place of Stillness more than ever, considering what had happened and what Irene had instigated.

This morning, Kath had woken up to the word KILLER on her white front door in dripping red spray paint. Why that word had been chosen was anyone's guess because Kath was no killer, and Billie had lived in a flat by herself for years, so why attack Kath? It was a ritual that had gone on for years—the residents wanted Kath to understand their intention: they didn't want the mother of a murderer in their midst, and the graffiti was the first step in getting her out.

"I'm sitting on the sand now," Kath said. "I want to talk about the things I told you when you arrived."

"Okay. Let's begin. How do you feel about moving from here and paying the mortgage on Billie's flat?" Janet asked.

"I think I'm going to have to do that. This lot down here have made themselves quite clear. It's funny, when it happens to someone else, you're just glad it isn't you, but I've never really put myself in other residents' shoes when Irene and her cronies do this."

"I remember it happening to Mrs Swan, do you?" Janet said. "Her only crime was being half Indian."

"I know. Bloody awful. I told Irene to leave off, but she wouldn't hear of it. I warned Swan what was going to happen, you know. Shit myself in case Irene found out I'd been helping the 'enemy' as she put it. God, this street, it's always been awful. Yes, it's time to go, like your mum did."

"Are you happy with that decision?"

"Yes, it feels like a weight's been lifted."

"Okay, the next issue. What are your thoughts on what Billie has done?"

"I'm going to fight to get her out of there. She's not a killer. It was the drugs. Billie's such a soft-hearted person; she'd never have hurt that little girl if she wasn't on some kind of trip. She's a nurse, for God's sake. I'm going to push until I find out who gave her that LSD."

Alarm poked Janet with a seriously sharp stick. She'd known Kath nearly all of her life, and the woman was persistent if nothing else. She'd dig and dig, unearth the truth somehow, and Janet couldn't let her.

"Sadly, the law will still see it that she killed someone, whether she intended to or not," Janet said. "It may have been under the influence, but she'll be expected to pay some kind of price. That tag is going to be attached to her for the rest of her life, regardless of how long she spends in prison."

"My poor girl…"

"Do you want to move on now?"

"Yes."

"Right, your third issue is how you're going to fund a television and media campaign."

"By selling this house and using the equity."

Charlene woke up. "Look, she's going to expose you if you're not careful. Are you seriously prepared for that to happen? Isn't it better that Billie stays in the nick for her whole sentence so she's out of the bloody way? There's no question she's going to get put down for a long stretch, and if it's twenty years or whatever, imagine the amount of damage Kath can do in that time."

"Good idea," Janet said to Kath. "But can you cope with all the finger-pointing, the abuse you'll get thrown your way?"

"I don't know. That's what I'm anxious about."

"Okay, let's go deeper to help you with that. If you stand and walk to the top of the dune, you'll see a beach hut." She paused to allow Kath to do that. "Do you see it?"

"Yes."

"Walk there in the sunshine. Feel the heat on your face. The peace surrounding you."

"Billie went here."

Janet stopped herself from panicking. Billie must have told her about that session. Fucking hell. "She did. Have you chatted to her about how much better she was coping without your husband after she went to the hut?"

"Yes. She said she was happier."

"She was. Our time in the hut will help you to cope with the days, months, and years ahead. To give you strength for Billie."

"Okay."

"What colour is your hut?"

"Pink with a yellow roof."

"Lovely. Does it have windows and a door?"

"One window beside a blue door."

"Open the door and go inside. There should be a sofa or a bed for you to lie on."

Kath sighed in wonder. "Oh, it's a four-poster."

"Very posh. Go and rest. Think of nothing but your breathing…"

By the time Kath came out of her safe place, she didn't want to help Billie anymore. Pleased with herself, Janet hid a smile.

"It's okay to change your mind," she said.

"Well, I have. Billie's a bitch for what she did to that kiddie. She ought to be ashamed of herself. Taking drugs and drinking, using that family's knife. Who does she think she is? I don't ever want to see her lying arse again."

"Do you want me to tell her? I'm going for a visit next week."

"No, she's phoning tonight. I'll tell her a few home truths. She'll know exactly where she stands by the time I'm done with her."

Janet sat opposite Billie in the visiting area. Eyes red raw, nails bitten, Billie looked a bloody state. Charlene preened over the devastation she'd caused, but a tiny part of Janet felt bad for the poor cow. If that tiny part was bigger, if she was a better person, this was the point she'd have confessed to what she'd done, but it was such a speck that it didn't even bear considering.

"I don't know why she's had such a sudden change of heart," Billie sniffled. "That call was awful. It was like someone else had told her what to say. The things she said…"

"Maybe Irene and that lot got to her," Janet suggested. "They did the spray-paint tactic on her door."

Billie stared at her with glassy eyes. "What did it say?"

"Killer."

"Oh God, poor Mum. None of this has anything to do with her."

"I know, but try telling Irene that. You know what they're like. Maybe your mum will come round, given time."

"I hope so. This has been a massive blow. She was going to help my legal team by giving the case exposure but..." She wiped her nose with her sleeve. "She's turned her back on me."

"All isn't lost. She said she's moving into your flat, so she can't hate you that much if she's keeping it on for you. I wish I could take you to the beach hut and make all these feelings go away, but I can't, not here."

"No, the guards would think we're up to something, and I need to be seen as a good person in here. I can't risk getting any black marks."

"If it's any consolation, I'll always be here for you."

"I'm surprised you are. I ruined everything for you with Sean."

"I don't blame him for wanting to stay with Whitney and help her through this," Janet said.

In truth, it pissed her off that Charlene's plan hadn't sent him running to Janet yet. She'd tried phoning him this morning, but he'd either blocked her number or changed his, and when she'd rung his work, the receptionist said he was taking a month off and wasn't receiving any messages from her.

Janet sighed. She'd wait for a while longer, and if he didn't come crawling back, she'd start a new experiment. In the meantime, she had Billie to manage. That would keep her occupied.

Chapter Eighteen

George sat in the corner at the back of The Water Wheel, his nerves frazzled at the thought of seeing Janet again in this kind of setting. It brought back too many memories of their nights out together, where they'd laughed and grown closer, much to his surprise. Maybe he shouldn't be so hard on himself. Maybe he *had* known something was off with her deep down, and he'd used the excuse of her trying to change him as a reason to ditch her.

Because he didn't want to face up to the fact that she was playing him.

He was a proud man, he was well aware of that, and how it sometimes had him unable to admit he could be wrong, yet he was happy to point it out to others when *they* were. The former wasn't a nice trait, and he'd try to fix that.

He liked things tied up in nice shiny bows, hating any threads left loose. To pretend their relationship had come to a natural end because he didn't like the way she'd turned into what amounted to a harpy was better than acknowledging his sixth sense had perhaps been bleating at him all along.

He needed to learn to listen to himself, regardless of whether he ended up looking a twat for taking the wrong path. So what if he made mistakes? He was human and entitled to cock up every now and then.

But I don't like cocking up.

He sipped his Coke and eyed the door, waiting for her to walk in as if she hadn't done anything wrong. And she hadn't, not really. It wasn't like *she'd* killed Emerald, was it. But the chat at the Taj had sprouted all manner of suspicious scenarios, and he couldn't shake the feeling that Janet had somehow had a big hand in that child dying.

Greg, in a long blond wig, beard, and hideous red-framed glasses, sat at the bar with a couple of Tick-Tock's men, ones Janet wouldn't recognise. They laughed at some joke or other, and to anyone watching, they were builders on a bender after a long day at work, their disguise even going as far as plaster dust speckling their clothes and splashes of paint here and there. Greg was close enough to listen in if he strained an ear, but George had a wire on tonight, and the conversation would go into Greg's earbud. Tick-Tock's men were here as a cover but also in case Janet went off on one and caused a scene. The extra muscle might come in handy if she turned into a wildcat and needed restraining.

The door swung inwards, and there she was, in a slim-fitting grey skirt suit, high heels, and her hair and makeup done all nice. Funny how she was no longer attractive to him, even though she was pretty. What was on the inside of Janet tainted what was on the outside—he found her ugly for trying to manipulate him, let alone all the other shit she'd got up to in the past.

She gave his table a quick glance, spotted he hadn't bought her a drink like he usually would, had the gall to roll her eyes, and made her way to the bar. She stood right next to Greg, oblivious, or so it seemed—now she'd spotted Ichabod outside her gaff, she might well have seen through Greg's disguise.

Time would tell.

She ordered a large glass of white wine—she must have got a taxi here—and paid using cash. Good, no digital record of her being here. She sipped, staring over the rim at George, and he stopped himself from showing his anger at her being pathetic. He had fifteen minutes down for this chat, so if she wanted to play at being a prick by wasting time, that was her problem.

She'd drunk half of the glass before she deigned to go over. Maybe she'd been listening to the builders' conversation to satisfy herself that one of them wasn't Greg. By the time she sat beside George, not opposite like she'd done in the past, he wanted to get up and walk out, conversation be damned, but he remained in place, if only to hear her made-up little tale as to why she hadn't been open with him. Was she sitting next to him so he couldn't see her face unless he turned to look at her?

"So why have you sent a skinny Irishman to spy on me?" she asked.

He stared ahead at the main door. "We regularly do updates on our employees and residents."

"Right, we're going with that story, are we? Okay." She sipped again. "That little story he told me earlier. It's very close to what happened in my past, but then you know that, don't you. What I don't understand is, why didn't you just ask me yourself?"

He gritted out through clenched teeth, "What I don't understand is, why didn't *you* tell me about it from the off?"

She shrugged. "I assumed you knew. After all, Clarke would have looked into me before you picked me as a therapist. I was aware of that. If I had something to hide, I'd have been shitting myself, wouldn't I? And I didn't. At no point did I give you reason to think I was dodgy."

George didn't trust himself to reply.

"Oh dear." She laughed. "He didn't tell you about Billie, did he."

George sighed. "What happened?"

"I suspect you already know. At least Janine came up trumps and you can trust her to pass on all information—that's what happened, isn't it? Your little piggy lapdog has been poking into me? Interesting as to why Clarke didn't, don't you think?"

The fact Clarke was dead and George couldn't torture him for yet another misdemeanour pissed him off. "Your tone's getting on my gonads."

"What tone?"

"It's smug, as if you're superior. Patronising."

She smirked. "Oh, I'm sorry. I wasn't aware I wasn't allowed to be any of those things. You really need to give me a list of do's and don'ts. There are so many rules, it's no wonder people forget them. Do this, do that. Don't do this, don't do that."

He imagined gripping her chin with his thumb and fingers and squeezing so hard he left bruises. Squeezing even harder and wrenching, dislocating her jaw. What the hell had he seen in her? "You just sound like a bitch, Janet, an unattractive one. You've got a few minutes left of this meeting, then I'm gone, so, what happened?"

"It's just like the file said. Billie killed my lover's daughter, end of."

"Why?"

"You'd have to ask her that. She's always said she didn't intend to do it. I believe her. She didn't even know the Dobsons before that party. She knew of Sean because I'd told her I was seeing him, and she knew he was married with a child, but other than that… Maybe she took it upon herself to kill Emerald to help me out, although that just isn't something she'd do. She's a caring person, a nurse, there's no way she'd want to murder anyone, let alone a kid. I think it's like the defence said. She had a bad trip on LSD, and for whatever reason, she stabbed Emerald."

"She used a knife from the family's kitchen."

"Yes, so it wasn't premeditated."

"You must have said something to her. Planted a seed."

Her irritating laugh tinkled. Like she thought she had the upper hand. Then she sobered. "Are you referring to 'Let the seed sprout'? If so, just say so, will you?"

"Yes, I was referring to that. What does it mean?" He hated having to ask her. Not having all the cards didn't sit well.

"How should *I* know?"

He wanted to wring her neck, force the info out of her. She *did* know, he sensed it. "Ichabod passed on your poncy excuse. You didn't tell us because it's too painful. You don't like talking or thinking about it. Yet you're gassing all right now."

"Because I don't have a choice. If I don't tell you, you'll get nasty. I know how it works, George. How *you* work. I answer your questions like a dutiful resident, you go off and contemplate my fate with your brother, and then I wait and see what that is, and if you decide I have to be *sorted*, I have to take it on the chin. All I've done is not tell you about a part of my past that I assumed you already knew. It's not my fault Clarke withheld the information, is it?"

Put like that, it all sounded a bit ridiculous, but something was still niggling him about this. "I'd have thought you'd have brought it up anyway."

"Is that what this is about? Your hurt pride? Christ, George, could you get any more egotistical? Don't even answer that."

"You think I'm poking into this because I've gone all diddum that you didn't tell me?"

"Aren't you?"

"Fuck off."

"The truth bites, doesn't it. Get over yourself. I'm entitled not to talk about a horrible period in my life, just the same as you are."

So it does *piss her off her that I never opened up.* "Not when it involves kids and their killers. That's something we'd need to know."

"Why? I didn't do anything."

She had an answer for everything, always had. Another bugging thing about her. They were too alike. Neither of them backed down in an argument. They were never going to work, and he'd been a prick to think they would.

"You lied to me about Philip," he said. "I've been told it was an arranged thing, you giving him that money was an investment, and the swindle wasn't in the way you made out. Was he even an ex? Or did you lie about that an' all?"

For the first time, her façade faltered. "You've been to see *Sean*?"

"So what if I have?"

"What did he tell you about me?"

Ah, so she is *capable of panic. There was me saying she wasn't.* "That's between me and him, but let's just say I'm aware I had a close shave with you. Thank fuck you ended it—then again, I was going to end it anyway, so I'd have been shot of you regardless."

"What. Did. He. Say?"

George was getting to her, and he held back a smile. "Nothing you need to be told. Why have you stayed friends with Billie?"

"Because she didn't mean to do it."

"If that's the case, why did you visit Randy Baker and tell him not to take on her case? Hardly the action of a good friend, is it."

"Because she still killed a child and shouldn't be let out until she's paid the price."

"Sounds to me like it was diminished responsibility. She shouldn't really be serving as long as she is. Or did you force her to kill Emerald?"

"*What?*"

"You heard me."

"Why would I do that? She was a little *girl*, for fuck's sake."

"You're getting riled up."

"Wouldn't you be if someone basically accused you of using a mate to kill someone?" She knocked back the rest of her wine. "Let's get to the nitty-gritty, seeing as you're so pressed for time. What are you going to do about me not opening up about that part of my past? Oh, and for lying about Philip, according to you."

"I haven't decided yet."

"Ah, you're still gathering information. I see." She stood. "Well, then, I'll just carry on with my life until you—"

Her phone rang. She dug it out of her bag. George caught a glimpse of the name on the screen, the first part HMP.

"Shit," Janet muttered. She sat again and answered, waiting a few moments to listen to whoever spoke. "It's okay that you're late calling, I understand there's a queue. No need to panic."

She sounded kind, a friend who had your back. George ground his teeth. She was a wolf in sheep's clothing, and Billie would do well to notice that.

"I did, yes." She glanced at George, pressing the phone tighter to her ear. "He's not interested in taking on your case. I'm so sorry." A pause. "Yes, I know what Freda said, but it seems she hasn't got any sway. He was adamant he's not doing it." She picked at lint on her skirt. "Please don't do the sheet. Please."

The sheet?

"I promise you, things will look better when you've had a sleep… No, Billie, I…" She held her phone in her lap and stared at it. "Shit. She hung up on me."

"Trouble in paradise?" George asked.

"Prison is hardly paradise, you unfeeling prick."

"It's not meant to be. It's designed to punish people."

"You should be in there," she said. "All the crap you've done."

Alarm bells rang. George had never had reason to think she'd grass him up before, but her saying that, well, it sent his skin cold, didn't it. She wasn't walking out of here alone tonight, she'd just sealed her fate. That had been an outright threat and, much as she'd deny it if he called her on it, he was going to listen to his gut. A surreptitious glance at Greg proved his twin was of the same mind—Janet could no longer be trusted with their secrets.

"Why did you visit Randy Baker twice?" he asked.

"What?"

"You were followed both times, but if you want to play out this charade for the last couple of minutes of this chat, that's fine."

She stuffed her phone away and hung her handbag over her body crossways. Drew the zip closed in a sharp movement. "How did they know it was me?"

"You're on about your disguise, I take it. Ichabod followed you from your place to the prison, then to Baker's. He took a picture of you, which I gave to Moon who saw you parked outside the PI's office. Why the need to hide behind a wig and glasses?"

"I'm not hiding. I do it because that's how Billie last knew me before she was put inside. She's got a thing about me moving on in life when she can't, so even me growing my hair, dying it, and using contacts instead of glasses would set her off."

"So you're being a good mate, is that it? Right…"

"It's clear you don't believe me."

"Nope, but I'll get to the bottom of it."

She stood again. "While you're doing that, I'll continue as normal, then."

"Except you won't, will you."

She stared down at him, her frown one from either genuine confusion or him getting on her last nerve. "What the fuck are you on about *now*?"

"That threat you just issued."

"Threat? What bloody threat?"

"That I should be in prison."

"What? Jesus, you're more paranoid than I thought."

"Maybe, but best to be safe than sorry."

"What's that supposed to mean?"

She glanced across as the bewigged Greg came to stand beside her.

"This is a private conversation," she snapped at him.

"Nah," Greg said. "I've been listening all along." He removed the earbud. "I don't like it when my brother gets threatened. It tends to rub me up the wrong way, know what I mean?"

She sighed. "I should have known. Just fuck off, Greg, will you? The pair of you." Her face hardened, and her irises darkened. "I tell you what, I'm sick of this. You two. The way you gad about. The way you expect people to just do what you want. You're bullies. You get off on hurting people. Janet's worth ten of you."

Greg laughed, but George stared at her.

She'd referred to herself in the third person.

"Janet?" he said.

She glared at him. "Yeah, Janet. I happen to care about her, and if you so much as lay a finger on her, I'll fucking have you. You've got *no* idea what I'm capable of."

Greg gripped the back of her neck. "Shut your weirdo mouth, because I'm sick of hearing your bastard voice. We're going to walk out of here, nice and calm, and you're going to spend the night on the rack. Any sudden moves and—"

She spun out of his grip, stood in front of him, and nutted him in the face. A shout went up from the builders. George stood and advanced, the shock of what she'd done, the audacity, sending his fist flying out to land on her temple. She went down to the floor on her knees, and George, ignoring his brother's bleeding nose, gripped her jacket and dragged her outside, adrenaline pulsing.

"You're going to regret doing that, you nutty fucking bitch," he said and hauled her along the pavement towards their BMW.

"Doing what?" She scrabbled for purchase, losing a shoe in the process. "What have I done?"

"Don't play innocent with me, Janet." He stopped dragging her and allowed her to stand, then marched her to the car. "Get the fuck in."

He threw her onto the back seat, and she landed awkwardly on her side. He reached in, sat her straight, put her safety belt on, and got in next to her, then straddled her lap. Hand clamped around her throat, the other braced on the back of the seat, he squeezed, Mad George coming for a visit, threatening to kill her. She grabbed his wrists to try to get him off her, but his strength outmatched hers. She gurgled, face puffing up, red, eyes bulging, and all he wanted to do was end her.

Self-preservation kicked in at the last minute— *CCTV cameras. Tick-Tock will have to get them wiped, people could be watching*—and he let her go, breathing heavily, getting off and flumping beside her, his anger so high he elbowed her in the nose to pay her back for likely breaking Greg's.

She screamed in pain and held her hands up to her face.

"You'll never get the chance to hit my brother again," he said. "Now sit there, shut the fuck up with that wheezing, and don't even look at me."

"Hit Greg?" she rasped out. "What do you mean?"

He ignored her, antsy for Greg to come out and drive them away. His twin appeared, all traces of blood gone—*he must have nipped to the gents*—although his nose seemed to have grown from the swelling and he had the makings of black eyes coming his way.

He got in the driver's seat and stared at George in the rearview: *You know what needs to be done, don't you, bruv.*

George nodded. "Just get us the fuck out of here."

The child locks clunked, the engine roared, and Greg peeled away.

"Oh God, no," Janet moaned. She sounded as if she'd smoked forty fags a day for years.

"Shut up," George snarled.

"Maggie… It was Maggie. She's back."

George didn't know who the hell Maggie was, and he didn't care. All he was interested in was stringing Janet up and teaching her a lesson before he got the information he needed from her.

Then took her life.

Chapter Nineteen

Billie sat in the recreation area with other women, waiting for Freda who'd promised to use her precious weekly call to phone Randy's mother. After the chat with Janet, Billie had told her what she'd said, and Freda was livid.

Why wasn't he taking on the case? It didn't make sense. Freda had been so sure he would. Billie had stupidly pinned all her hopes on it, it had been a beam-sweeping lighthouse in the sea, showing her the way to safety, to freedom. Unless Freda came back with good news, there was nothing for it. Billie would use the sheet when she wasn't on watch. How long that would be, she didn't know, but she'd been put in a new cell with a camera in the top-right corner, and guards observed her at all times when she wasn't in it during her working, eating, or recreation hours.

At least she still had those. She'd go stir crazy if she was treated like she was in solitary. If only she hadn't written that letter to Janet, basically shouting from the rooftops what she planned to do. She should have waited until a visit, whispered it instead.

No use crying over spilt milk, as Mum used to say.

Recalling that hurt. Anything to do with Mum hurt.

A guard stared at Billie, a burly man with black stubble who looked like he'd been on the bevvies last night; his eyes had that gritty appearance to them. Billie used to love getting lashed up, staggering from pub to pub, pissed as a fart and laughing with Janet. She'd only gone to the Dobsons' house that day because Janet had wanted to give Emerald a present. She'd lost count of the amount of times she wished she'd never gone. She hadn't been feeling that great, had told Janet she wasn't at her best so should stay home, a tad low for some reason but, as usual, her friend had cajoled her.

Billie had gone because she'd owed Janet for all those free therapy sessions she'd given her after Dad died in that accident at work. He'd fallen from high scaffolding, breaking his back and neck, his head cracking open like a fucking boiled egg. Billie had lost it, couldn't function, and Janet had saved her. She'd helped Mum, too.

The thought of Mum soured Billie's mood even further. She knew Billie better than anyone yet had still cast her aside. How could she believe Billie would have *chosen* to kill that little girl? She'd said she'd never forgive Billie for going into the bathroom and stabbing Emerald, that the drug defence was a load of old rubbish, Billie's way of trying to wriggle out of punishment.

Why would she even *think* that?

How come Mum had changed her opinion of Billie so drastically—and quickly? If Billie didn't know better, she'd say Janet had a hand in that, seeing as she'd gone to see Mum the day before the scheduled prison visit. She hated thinking these things about her friend, but like she'd told her, being in here had her imagining all sorts.

No, Janet wouldn't have poisoned Mum's mind. Why would she do that when she'd supported Billie from the start? Or, was it like Billie had contemplated once, that because Janet's mum had moved away then died, she was using Billie's as a substitute and didn't want to share the affection?

She let her mind wander to that day Janet had found the fiver and they'd scoffed all those sweets and crisps. Memories like that usually kept her going, but today, it only served to bring it home how stuck she was. She'd never go on a roundabout again, never laugh her head off with her friend until she couldn't breathe. Her life had ended the moment she'd been sent here.

The guard continue to stare, and, tempted to poke her tongue out at him but opting not to, Billie made out he didn't faze her and watched the telly, proving that his gaze on her wasn't a problem. It was. She imagined him seeing into her soul, knowing her thoughts, and it unsettled her. She *had* to get off watch, and she'd do whatever it took to achieve that, so she'd play the good girl until they decided she wasn't a suicide risk. She'd write another letter to Janet and make out everything here was fine, she'd stopped thinking horrible things, and she planned to start a new education course to keep her occupied.

From the corner of her eye, she caught sight of Freda coming in. She didn't dare turn to look at her—she didn't want to see her expression of resignation until she had to. Just a minute or so more of hope, that wasn't too much to ask, was it? She envisaged Baker agreeing to help her after all, the new trial going her way, and outside, on the court steps, she'd thank Janet, Freda, Baker, and her legal team for sticking by her. She'd apologise to the Dobsons, staring directly at the camera so they'd see the sincerity in her eyes.

All too soon, Freda sat beside her. The time for fairy stories was over, she sensed it. Only the stark truth was coming her way now.

Billie waited for the guillotine to fall. If her nerves got any worse, she'd have a panic attack, she knew it. She breathed in and out deeply, nice and steady, telling herself her options were simple: No help, she'd take herself out of this world. Help, and she'd fight another day.

"I got hold of her," Freda said. "It's not good news, I'm afraid."

Billie imagined what it would be like when the ripped-up length of sheet pressed against her windpipe. How her weight pulling on it might snap her neck, her death coming quickly. Would it be painful? Would she effectively suffocate? How long would she suffer for? Would it be like Bella in the next cell had said, that she'd instinctively claw at the sheet to free herself, even though she wanted to die? Bella's victim had done that, and she'd watched him die, smiling.

God, get me out of here, away from these insane people.

"Go on, then," Billie said on a sigh. "You may as well tell me everything."

"His mum said he'd phoned her not long ago. Told her not to talk to me about you anymore. That no matter what she says to him, how much she begs, he's not helping you, and she needs to keep her nose clean else Moon will have something to say about it."

Billie frowned, confused. "What's Moon got to do with it?"

"He paid Randy a visit, as did some other bloke. Irish."

"I don't understand. Why are they getting involved?"

"Look, I told you I don't like Janet. There's something about her that's iffy—I can't put my finger on it, but she's strange. And how weird is it that you told her about Randy, she goes to see him to supposedly check him out for you, then Moon and the Irish fella went there, too? Something's not right."

Had Billie's subconscious been warning her about Janet all along since she'd been in here? There had been so many times Janet had said something or other on visits that had given Billie pause.

"I'm sorry, mate," Freda went on. "I don't understand it. Randy's usually such a nice fella, but I suppose when Moon turns up, you've got to do as you're told. I'm actually surprised he hasn't got someone in here to do me over, seeing as I've been accused of killing that old biddy on his estate—which, as you know, I didn't."

Billie didn't show her devastation, and she didn't have the energy to go into a chat about how innocent Freda was. How rude of Freda to even bring that up at a time like this. Freda was as selfish as Janet had said she was if she grabbed at any chance to talk about her own situation.

Billie schooled her features. The guard would still be watching, and he'd see her change of demeanour, so she put on a smile. Freda would understand why. They all pretended in here.

"Maybe Moon believes I did it on purpose, like my mum does." Billie folded her arms.

"It was the drugs," Freda said. "Anyone can see that. Don't lose heart, love. We can find someone else. His mum said she'd have a look for another investigator who does stuff free until the money comes in."

"Thanks." Billie remembered what Janet had said about Freda having her on. "Did you really phone your friend?"

"Eh?" Freda crossed her ankles in front of her. "Of course I bloody did. Why would you ask something like that? I said I'd ring her and I did. I'm not in the habit of lying. What put that in your head?"

"It's just Janet. She said at the last visit that you might be pulling a fast one to stop me from, you know, doing something to myself. Like, you'd be lonely without me here." Billie prayed for a good answer to that—maybe if someone showed they cared about her, she might stick around, despite the direness of her life.

"What?" Freda whispered and glanced over her shoulder to check if the women behind were listening. "I know you're on watch, but fucking hell, I didn't realise you actually meant it when you said about...that thing. We all get down days, and I assumed you were having one. I genuinely want to help you. You're young, you don't want to spend the best years of your life stuck in here. I'm older, I've had my fun, but you? No, you shouldn't even be in here."

Billie felt better now. Freda cared.

It might not be enough, though. Another dark day could come, much blacker than all the others put together, swamping her, and Billie might not be able to push through it.

She continued to stare at the telly. "No one's going to take it on, you know that, don't you. Everyone thinks I did it and used drugs as an excuse."

"But we have to try. If it works for you, maybe they'll help me next. I swear to you, I didn't kill that woman. Someone else working there must have done it and blamed me."

Billie finally looked at her, annoyed once again that Freda had turned the focus onto herself, but she said what was on her mind anyway. "Thanks, Freda."

"What for?"

"Giving a shit."

"It's what friends do, mate."

I'm still going to end it. I can't go on like this.

Billie's whole body filled with nerves. It was one thing to contemplate ending her life, but to be presented with the starkness of it really happening was another matter. Her legs jiggled, she couldn't keep them still, and her teeth chattered.

Freda placed a hand on Billie's knee. "Bloody hell, pack it in, will you? What's up with you? Do you need to go to the bathroom?"

Billie stopped jiggling.

Everything inside her head clouded.

Freda stared at her in shock.

Billie couldn't stop herself. She lunged.

Chapter Twenty

Janet couldn't stop shaking. Seeing George like this, being at the end of his brand of justice, a hand around her neck... She'd imagined it many times but had never seen him go so far into anger that he'd hurt her. He'd told her all about it, the things he'd done, the emotions he'd experienced while doing it, all in the name of therapy, and she'd been fascinated to study someone who had the balls to do what *she* wanted to do. What the voices urged her to do. They could have been a murderous duo eventually, but she wasn't stupid, there was no getting out of this now.

She'd just told him Maggie was back, but George wouldn't believe her if she expanded on that and explained further. That there was a Maggie and a Mad sitting side by side in the back of a BMW would be hard for him to fathom, that his former lover was actually suffering from Dissociative Identity Disorder, that somehow, fate had thrown them together on the day he'd walked into her office for help.

Except she wasn't Maggie now, she was Janet, and Mad appeared to be Just George, although that flexing of his jaw said otherwise. Confused, frightened of what was in her future, and not being sure *who* he was at the minute had her leaning her head back and closing her eyes to work out which personality lived inside her now.

Her throat hurt from being throttled, and hot tears burned at the fact he'd even had the urge to kill her. She'd thought she meant more to him. Thought she'd got under his skin enough to leave an imprint that meant it would always give him pause when it came to her. Maybe, because of that imprint, Mad had to take over because Just George couldn't bring himself to hurt her. That must have been why Maggie had made an appearance in The Water Wheel—to save Janet from being upset more than she'd already been.

Janet had gone into her usual self-preservation mode from the off, taking her time buying a drink, watching out for people in disguise to pounce on her any second. She should have known, with the amount of stress she'd been under, that she might not be able to control Maggie. She'd fought it, the change, the *snap*. When it had become clear George knew more than she'd bargained for, Janet had panicked. Maggie had tapped on her shoulder, and, as if Janet straddled both personalities at once, something that had never happened before, Maggie had said to George: *"You should be in there. All the crap you've done."*

And she'd known, fuck, she'd known he would take it the wrong way. Maggie didn't know him well enough to realise how he'd have perceived that. The last thing Janet recalled saying before she found herself outside, being dragged to the car, was: *"Just fuck off, Greg, will you? The pair of you."* Whatever had happened in between was lost to her, although she now had a good idea. Maggie had head-butted Greg, and Janet would pay the price for it. Hurting him was a massive no-no, and she wouldn't be able to get herself out of any punishment without explaining that she and George shared the same issue.

He'd never buy it. He'd say she was making it up to get herself out of the shit.

She had to try, though. To save herself, talk him round, get him back in her bed.

She stared out of the window. Greg had pulled up to some metal gates.

They were at the warehouse.

"George, please…"

"Don't fucking 'George, please' me. It's gone way past that." He gripped her wrist so tight the skin burned.

It's Dad all over again. "You're hurting me."

"That's the idea."

Greg got out, opened the gates, then got back in to drive into a car park of sorts. He released the child locks and left the car again to secure the gates. Then he entered the warehouse, glancing over his shoulder, probably his instinct nudging him to check if George was all right. Their bond, their caring for one another, their *devotion*, twisted something inside Janet. Jealousy. Envy. She'd never been loved like that apart from Mum, and if things went the usual way once she was inside that building, she never would.

"We can work this out," she said. "If you just let me explain..."

He let go of her wrist as if he couldn't stand to touch her. "Explain what? I thought you'd said all you had to say in the pub. Or have you been lying again, keeping something back?"

"It isn't like you think. You'd understand if you put yourself in my shoes."

"I *never* want to stand in your shoes, thanks. There's more to that murder than you're letting on. You may as well just tell me you had a bigger part in it, because I know you did. Something's nagging at me to find out what it is. And I will."

"You're getting agitated. Do you need to go to The Place of Stillness?" If she could just get him there, she could change all this. Change his *mind*. Warp it to think what *she* wanted it to think with regards to her. Unethical, and wholly wrong, but...

"Desperate times call for desperate measures, Janet."

"The Place of Stillness?" He turned to stare at her. "With *you*? Fuck right off."

"I'm scared you're going to kill me, so if I could just help you to calm down…"

"Calm down? *Calm down*? I don't *want* to fucking calm down. Why d'you think we've brought you here, for a fucking Mad Hatter's tea party? This is serious, Janet, as serious as it gets. This is the *end*, do you understand?"

She'd never thought this would happen to her. Charlene's arrogance had carried her though any iffy spots in life, yet the bitch had deserted her now there was no chance of luring George to the dune. To the beach hut. Janet would have to negotiate this on her own, and she wasn't sure she was strong enough. She knew what happened in that warehouse, had revelled in George's tales of the goings-on, wishing she'd been there to watch him kill people, all the while making out she thought it was abhorrent. She was so broken it was unreal, and she'd thought, if she had George as her permanent stability, she could live through him to assuage her need to do exactly what he did—murder and run roughshod over people.

She shouldn't have gone into her profession in order to work out what was wrong with her. She wouldn't have had to study herself and thousands of people, then. She'd never have known that her main self, Janet, was called the 'host', Charlene and Maggie were 'alters', and that together, all parts of her were called a 'system'—they were all slices of one personality that didn't work in tandem as a whole. Instead, she should have gone to the doctor, asked for help. Studied something else at uni. Become someone else.

But then she'd never have met George and wouldn't be here now, and although she should have massive regrets, she *didn't* regret the path she'd chosen. She'd known love with Sean—or infatuation—and she'd known love with George, although, she could admit now, that was also infatuation on her part and neither man had actually *loved* her, not like she'd wanted.

That need to be cared for despite her personality disorder had pushed her down this path. Instead of wedding bells and convincing George to let her join him on his torture sprees, she was here, sitting in the back of a car.

Facing death.

Maggie had been successful and had managed to come back a second time. Her brief visit earlier in the pub had been too fleeting for her liking, and once Janet had been secured to a spiked rack on the wall of some shitty warehouse, stressed to her eyeballs, Maggie had broken through again. She had to take over, Janet was in no fit state to do so, and it had been so long since Maggie had done this for any length of time it felt as if she'd broken out of stasis.

To lie dormant, to be so suppressed there was no chance of escape, had been frustrating to say the least. Charlene was so strong-willed, stubborn, and single-minded that she'd been able to keep Maggie locked up, what with having Janet on her side as well. Still, Maggie was out now, and those bloody twins had a few home truths coming their way. She'd heard all about them from Janet—she and Janet weren't as separate as Janet liked to think. Fair enough, Janet didn't know when Maggie had paid a visit until it was too late, but Maggie kept tabs on Janet, Charlene, and everything they got up to.

Being naked didn't faze Maggie, she revelled in it, although Janet had been mortified upon being stripped, despite George having seen every inch of her in the past. She hadn't coped with Greg getting an eyeful of her assets, so it was just as well she wasn't here. Janet lay sleeping inside Maggie, too traumatised to even poke her head out.

George paced in front of her. What *did* he look like in that white getup? Who did he think he was, one of those forensic coppers? Christ, his arrogance knew no bounds. Thank God Janet had ended it with him. It would have been awful to have him more permanently in their lives. *And* that manky brother of his, the jealous little shit.

Greg sat on a wooden chair facing her, and he thumbed a message on his phone. It pinged with a response. "Tick-Tock's sorting the cameras and whatever."

"Good." George slapped a cricket stump on his gloved palm.

Was that supposed to scare her?

Maggie chortled.

"I don't know what you find so fucking funny," George snapped.

"You, playing the hardman," Maggie said. "You just look a complete dick, though. One of those milk bottle sweets on legs."

"You should know insults don't bother me, Janet."

"I'm Maggie. And leave her out of this."

"D'you know, I reckon Ichabod was right. You *are* off your rocker. Is that why you gravitated to me? A kindred spirit an' all that?"

"Janet wanted to help you, fuckface, and what did you do? Accused her of not knowing her shit. She knows exactly what she's talking about, I'll have you know."

"What, all that DID crap?"

"It isn't crap. Mad George is the same as me — the one who takes over. We're the ones who make you and Janet lose complete control."

"Why are you talking about yourself like that?" He slapped the stump again.

"Like what?"

"Like you're not Janet."

"Because I'm *not* her, that's why. Jesus, get with it, will you?"

George's eyebrows rose. *"She's* a DID sufferer?"

"Well, I wouldn't call it suffering, but she might. It's hard work keeping me out of the way, she reckons."

George narrowed his eyes, as if he knew something Maggie didn't. "According to her, she wouldn't know you existed unless she did something as you and someone told her about it. Is that what happened? Did she realise what was going on? Has she been diagnosed and hides it from everyone?"

"*Self*-diagnosis. Fuck me, do you think she'd be stupid enough to go to a doctor and admit there's three of us?"

"Three?" His mouth dropped open.

Maggie, smug that she knew everything and he didn't, offered a nod. "The other one, that's who she calls Charlene. She's the clever clogs who got inside Billie's head."

George stopped pacing. "By doing what?"

"Let the seed sprout." Maggie laughed. This bloke was thick as pig shit; he knew sod all, yet he acted as if he held all the cards. "Turn that frown upside down, Georgie Porgie, it makes you look uglier than you already are."

He shook his head as if her insult didn't bother him. "What does that mean? The seed thing."

"Wouldn't you like to know."

"Err, I do actually, else I wouldn't have fucking asked, would I, you dumb bitch."

"Ooh, resorting to name-calling. Funny how you tell people it's a pointless exercise, then you do it yourself. But that's always been your way, hasn't it, do as I say, not as I do. You're pathetic. Nothing but a windbag filled with a sense of his own importance."

"Don't hold back, will you."

"I don't intend to." Maggie shouldn't say it, Janet wouldn't like it, but she would anyway… "Why she didn't plant the seed in *your* head when she took you to the dunes, I'll never know."

"What?" He'd roared it, his eyes ablaze, spittle flying.

"Fucking Nora, mate, keep your hair on. No need to get aerated, is there."

He walloped her knees with the stump. Sharp pain flowered, but she breathed through it. If this was all he had to offer her by way of punishment, she'd take it.

"I'm not your fucking mate, sunshine."

"Ah, Mad is on his way. Oh goody." If she could have rubbed her hands together, she would. She had so much to say to this prick on

Janet's behalf. It was about time he heard the truth. "Janet's got the ability to end you. She can take you to that dune, then get you to walk past it to where all the fun happens. There's a beach hut, and she told Billie to go in there and close her eyes, have a nice sleep, and when she woke up, all her worries about her dead dad would be gone. It wasn't a lie, she did help Billie out there, but it was the other thing she did that was a classic."

Greg stood, shoving his hands in his suit trousers pockets. "What's she on about dunes and beach huts for?"

"Doesn't matter," George said, sheepish.

Maggie smiled. "Oh, what a wonderful revelation! You don't share *everything* with your brother. Didn't you want him to know you visit The Place of Stillness when you're with Janet? Why? Scared he'll think you've turned hippy or something? That you're into all that mumbo-jumbo stuff?"

George whacked her around the face with the stump.

Maggie grinned though the pain, but fucking hell, her cheek hurt, and wet heat travelled in a line down her skin. Blood.

"What happened in the beach hut?" he shouted.

"Be nice and I'll tell you."

"Don't tell me what to do, woman. I swear to God, if you don't explain…"

The pinch of aches brewed in her armpits from where her wrists had been secured to the upper corners of the rack, and the spike ends dug into her back. Trying to bow it to keep away from the sharp tips was hard work. Maybe he'd let her get down if she fed him a few titbits. She doubted it, but it was worth a try. Poor Janet didn't deserve to come back to her body any sorer than it already was.

"That's where seeds are planted. You have no idea how close she was to taking you there. She's got this ledge, one she's shit scared of falling over, because when she does, she's fucked because I come along. Or Charlene, which is more likely. We get her to do things she's too afraid to do. I'd have bloody loved watching her telling you to kill yourself. There'd have been words, ones you'd have heard at some point after she'd brought you out of the safe place, and they'd have triggered you. Billie's was: *Do you need to go to the bathroom*?"

Maggie roared with laughter. It felt so good to see the look on George's face, to know he was piecing it all together and coming up with the truth, a truth Janet had successfully hidden for years.

George strode over to the table, threw the stump down, and brought over a circular saw. He stood in front of her and stared up, hatred in his eyes, revving the tool a few times, probably to scare her witless. If she was any judge, she'd say Mad was prodding him to kill her. Part of her wanted to goad him, but the other part, the one that cared about Janet, told her to tone it down a bit. It was all well and good playing games with him, but the objective here was to get him to understand how Janet would be an asset to them. She could take so many people to the beach hut, make them killing machines for the twins. They'd become an unstoppable trio.

"She's not going to go for that, Maggie."

"Oh, fuck off, you."

George stopped revving the saw. "Who are you telling to fuck off?"

Maggie realised her mistake. "I wasn't talking to you."

"Who *were* you talking to, then?"

"Charlene."

"What the fuck?" he muttered, but it seemed as if he understood.

Did *he* have a third person? Maggie couldn't recall if Janet had mentioned it. Maybe he'd successfully hidden the third from her, but it was so *interesting* if another alter lived inside him, too. Who was it? What did the third get up to? Was he Charlene's equivalent?

"What's the matter, George?" she asked.

"Nothing. Why did you get Billie to kill that kid?" he said through gritted teeth.

"I didn't! That was Charlene. Fucked if I'm taking the blame." She sighed. "And work it out, will you? The kid was a stumbling block. Sean wouldn't do what Janet wanted with her around."

"So you...Janet...got rid of her? Or was that this Charlene bint?"

She mentally clapped. "Give the pleb a medal for finally working it out."

He raised the saw and held the blade at her ankle.

"Oh dear, George, you're not thinking straight." She flashed her teeth at him. "If you kill me, you kill Janet, and if you kill Janet, you'll

have no proof she used Billie to commit murder —
if you tortured *her* enough, she'd spill the beans."
She tilted her head. "Then again, can you risk
letting Janet tell the police all about you two? I
doubt your copper could cover *that* up. So you
have a quandary. Kill all three of us to save
yourselves and your brother—or let Janet live
and set the wheels in motion to free what's
essentially an innocent woman."

George kept the blade where it was. "Talk to
me, bruv."

He's losing it. He needs his brother to ground him.
Fascinating.

Greg stared at Maggie. "End her. *Now.*"

Chapter Twenty-One

Slicing up a former lover as Just George, no Mad in sight, no Ruffian to lend a helping hand, was a boring experience. Yes, he was angry at what Janet—or whoever the fuck she was at the time—had done, what she'd manipulated Billie to do, but slicing through her belly, her spine, the blade grating on the bottom of a spike, didn't give him the satisfaction he needed—what he'd *expected*.

He felt cheated.

And guilty he'd saved his selves and his twin over helping Billie.

You promised Sean you'd end Billie. That still needs to be done. Saving her was never an option.

Janet's bottom half had flopped forward and thudded onto his chest, her ankles attached to the manacles, blood gushing, soaking through his forensic suit and his grey one beneath, her arse pitted with small holes from the spikes. He stepped back to let it fall all the way and studied her top half. Blood spatter decorated her skin, a droplet of scarlet hanging off one nipple. She'd died with her head down, eyes closed, and she appeared to be asleep, no semblance of being in pain visible. Whoever Janet had been during that conversation wasn't anyone George would want in his life—in anyone's life.

Christ, all those people he'd exposed to her.

"How many others has she planted seeds in?" he wondered.

Greg came to stand beside him. "Fuck knows."

"We could have people turning nutty if someone says phrases to them, the ones that trigger them."

"Maybe she only did it with Billie."

George swallowed. "What if she was lying, saying she wanted to do it to me but hadn't yet. What if she *has*? What if I hear a few words and go off and top myself?"

"You won't. We'll go and see some other therapist who can do something to counteract it. Did you even know she could do hypnotherapy?"

"Not like that." He explained about the safe place. "That's sort of like it, except I have control there, I can come back anytime I want. I know because I've done it."

"Did you ever go to the beach hut? That you know of?"

"No."

Greg patted him on the shoulder then walked off to drag the stepladder over. "Good. We'll get her down, cut her up, and ditch the fucking slag."

They got on with it, George lost in his head, unnerved there might be a ticking bomb inside it that he wasn't even aware of. The only emotion he felt while slicing her into pieces was anger that she'd used that poor cow, Billie, to kill a child, and that Emerald had lost her life in some sick game. How many lives had that ruined? How many people woke up empty every single day without that little girl's laughter to listen to?

"I didn't see it in her," he said. "I should have seen it."

"Nobody did, so don't bother beating yourself up about it. If anyone asks, we'll say she's moved away. We'll get a new therapist, in a new place, then Aster's still got a job. It'll all work out, trust me."

"You're the only one I *do* trust one hundred percent."

"Same."

They bagged the body parts up, and Greg took them out the back to dump them in the river. George worried about whether Janet had kept a dossier on them—he'd send men round to her place, and her office, and remove everything inside them. They'd be destroyed by fire, including her computer and laptops. Her phone. Her car. Everything that was Janet would be gone.

Then there was Billie. He'd tip Janine off as to what his plans were. He'd find someone to kill

Billie inside; Janine's guard in there could help root someone out to do it.

That means fucking up someone's life, though. Getting them to murder her. Manipulating them.

It left a sour taste in George's mouth as it had strains of what Janet had done.

Greg came back having dumped the last of the bag contents. "Shit, you've got that look about you. What have you been thinking?"

George told him.

Greg shook his head. "No, we don't involve innocent people in this. That's what created this mess in the first place."

"Then what do we do about Billie? Leave her to rot?"

"I don't know. Let me have a think."

George nodded. Pent-up energy floated inside him, and it was inevitable he was going to go off on his own later, as Ruffian, while Greg was asleep. The disgust inside him had to go somewhere, and if he took it out on some scumbag or other who deserved it, he'd feel better.

Or feel something better than *this* anyway.

Janet knowing about Ruffian creeped him out. What if Charlene or Maggie had taken over and followed him after their dates? What if she'd filmed him as Ruffian or taken pictures?

All the more reason to destroy her belongings.

It had been difficult to talk with Greg there, to get answers, and George had tried to think of an excuse to get him to leave, but Greg would have wanted to know why, and then Maggie could have opened her mouth and revealed things he'd told Janet, private things, thoughts and needs he'd only ever told her. Yes, he shared almost everything with Greg, but the softest parts of him, no, and that was why it hurt so much to be betrayed by Janet. Her saying he deserved to go to prison—she'd implied she'd reveal all, get him done for every murder, every act of violence, every torture, yet she'd claimed to care about him.

Confused by why it still upset him, he had a strong word with himself. He'd learnt a valuable lesson by being involved with Janet, and the only option going forward was to avoid women like the plague until he knew them inside out. If he had any desire to find love and get married later down the line, it would be to someone he'd known for a while. A friend first, for a long while, then they could move on to bigger things.

But at the minute, the thought of being with *anyone* like that sent a shiver through him.

He was better off alone.

With Mad and Ruffian for company.

The phone jangling stopped Ruffian just as he was about to get into their pretend work van in the garage. He went into the kitchen via the connecting door, checked the screen, then answered.

"What's got you ringing us at three in the fucking morning?"

Janine tutted. "You told me earlier to keep you abreast of anything to do with Billie. My mate in the nick, the guard I told you about, has just let me know she offed someone called Freda earlier."

The hairs on Ruffian's arms stood on end. "You what?"

"Hmm. She threw her to the floor and strangled her. Word has it she was wild. Like she was possessed or something. Not that the guard would outright admit it, but they might have held back on trying to pull Billie away because it meant Freda got her just deserts for what she'd done to that old woman and Billie will have to serve extra time."

"Shit a brick."

"I know. Regardless of you telling me she was forced to kill that nipper, she can't claim innocence on this one. There's no way we can get to her now. She's in solitary."

He sighed. "Christ. I wonder what made her do it. Was there a row or something? Maybe she went ballistic because Baker isn't taking her case on."

"That was discussed. One of the other women listened to their convo prior to Billie losing the plot. The weird thing is, the last thing Freda said to her isn't the sort of thing to get up in arms about."

"What did she say?"

"She put her hand on her knee and asked her if she needed the bathroom."

Ruffian's blood ran cold. "Fuck."

"What's up?"

He explained everything. "So now I'm paranoid she's done it to me, put some little phrase in my head that will set me off."

"Go and see someone. Get them to sort you out."

"Will do. Anyway, cheers for letting me know."

"Night-night."

"Night."

He cut the call, took off his Ruffian disguise, and locked the door to the garage. Any killing to make him feel better would have to wait. The news had sickened him, scared him if truth be told. The thought that just one phrase could set someone off was hard to get his head around. Such a simple phrase, too, one used by many people. It could have been said any number of times since Emerald's murder, yet miraculously, Billie hadn't heard it, or if she had, it hadn't triggered her.

What were the odds of that?

Or was it the hand on the knee? Those two things combined?

In his boxer shorts, as George, he went upstairs to break the news to Greg, and until he'd seen another therapist to undo what might have been done to him, he didn't want anyone touching him, not even his twin.

Fuck that.

Chapter Twenty-Two

The therapist, a man this time, Vic Collins, had given up work for the NHS and settled well in the new premises. Aster had said he was a nice bloke, kind and caring, no acerbic side to him like Janet had shown. Sixty-two, hair greying, his portly body going to seed, Vic was a hit with everyone who went to see him, including George, who hadn't revealed anything nefarious and kept their chats to mental health issues. Having been burnt once, he wasn't prepared to put all his eggs in one basket again.

Of course, Vic knew who the twins were, what they did, and a thorough police check by Janine revealed he had nothing more to his name than a parking ticket back in eighty-three. His wife had died six years ago, and with no children, he was the ideal candidate. With his wages tripled and a home provided, he was as amenable as they come, and George was ninety percent sure the bloke was on the level.

The chat about what would happen to Vic if he crossed them had helped.

Vic had done a similar thing to Janet, taking George to a safe place, but this time, it was of George's choosing. That went some way to alleviating his nerves as he'd sat on the comfy counselling chair with his eyes closed during his first session last week, waiting for Vic to fix him, which he had, telling George that whatever trigger had been planted in him was to be ignored.

At no point had George lost consciousness, as far as he could tell. He'd chosen the old kitchen of his childhood for the safe space—odd, considering that house had been filled with terror and anxiety, violence, harsh words, fists flying — but it was the table he sat at with a Pot Noodle and tiger bread in front of him that represented the safety. Those times, when Mum had pushed the boat out if she had spare cash, producing the noodle pots from her string shopping bag, had been the best of his childhood. For that speck of time, with no Richard at home, his fake father at the pub sinking pint after pint, George had felt secure.

He was there now, in a third session with Vic. Mum stood leaning against the sink unit, her arms folded, watching him wolf down the treat. He glanced over at her, and it was as if he were truly there, the sun shining on her hair through the kitchen window, burnishing it, turning her into the angel she was. She'd made some questionable decisions in her life, no getting away from it, but she'd done the best she could with the hand she'd been dealt.

Tears burned. He wanted to get up, cuddle her, smell her familiar Mum smell, for her to stroke his back and say, "It'll be all right, son, you'll see." He could do that, he could, and in the limbo state he was in, he'd actually feel her warmth, her arms around him, her breath ruffling his hair as she spoke. But to do that would be too painful, too real, and it would only torment him with the fact that it *wasn't* real.

"How do you feel, George?" Vic asked gently.

"I want my mum," he blurted, and fuck, the tears spilled, hot on his cheeks.

"Why don't you go to her, then?"

"Because it'll hurt. It'll remind me of what I don't have anymore."

"But it could also heal. Give you what you sorely require. You miss her, you need her, so why not take what's on offer while you can? You might not see her so clearly next time. You might not get the chance again. Some people long for this, one last touch. Do you really want to squander it?"

George got up from the kitchen table and walked towards his mother, but talking to Vic had broken the spell, and she faded, the loaf of bread behind her on the worktop visible through her disappearing body. He rushed to her before it was too late, her hand reaching out, him grasping it, and he willed himself to *feel* it, to get some kind of energy from her. It was there, faint but there, and it seemed as if the contact had stilled the raging waters inside him. That she was telling him it was okay to make mistakes—she'd made them with Richard and Cardigan, and he'd made one with Janet, and countless others with himself.

But most of all, he felt love, peace, and that was enough.

George left Vic's office and approached the reception desk. He was desperate for more of those emotions so wanted to make another appointment. He needed his mother during his healing process, and as he couldn't achieve that state on his own, he'd be seeing Vic often until he felt he could manage again by himself with Greg as a prop.

If he'd learnt one thing from Janet, it was that he needed a therapist to keep him on track. She'd been good in some ways, he couldn't dispute that, but in others...

Fucking monster.

"All right, Aster?" He placed his palms on the desk and smiled at her, then glanced at the closed office door. What he'd really asked was: *Everything okay with Vic?*

"It's bloody wonderful," she said, then whispered, "Nothing to report here."

He whispered back, "Not even people querying about Janet?"

"They seem to have swallowed the story."

Aster was one of the very few who knew what had happened. George trusted her, as much as he could allow himself to trust anyone other than Greg, and they needed her to know so she could redirect people's thoughts on the matter of their former therapist abandoning ship without saying goodbye. Vic had explained that the relationship between a patient and their therapist was often a strong bond for the client, and Janet waltzing off the way she had could have a detrimental effect, one Vic aimed to mend in anyone who chose to see him instead.

"Good. If anything crops up, no matter how small, you know where I am." He pushed off the desk. "I need another appointment for next week."

She tapped on the keyboard. "He's fully booked, which doesn't surprise me because he's *that* good, but you can have one of his emergency appointments—like I can say no to you anyway." She smiled.

"Cheers."

He said his goodbyes and left the building, a cottage that had once been a pub down one of the streets behind The Angel. Vic lived in the rear rooms and upstairs, using the front for business.

George got in the BMW and drove to Ichabod's. In the three months since Janet's departure from the world, George had visited the Irishman frequently and, dare he say it, they'd become friends of sorts. The bloke had proved his worth ten times over and was now on a par with Will and Martin, the twin's most trusted.

George thought about the file that had been found on Janet's personal laptop. The nutbag had kept all the clippings about the murder and trial, as if she saw herself as some kind of serial killer who needed trophies. The letters from Billie had upset him—the poor cow really hadn't known what she'd done, and another visit to Sean, to show them to him, meant the grieving father had found it in his heart to forgive her. George wasn't sure he'd be the bigger man like that if he stood in his shoes, but the remorse she'd felt regarding Sean and his wife had shone through.

He parked, thinking about his dreamlike encounter with Mum, how he was feeling so calm—and generous. It had come to him, when she'd held his hand, that he ought to sort Ichabod out with a better gaff now he and Greg had plans for the fella. His studio flat at the top of a run-down house wasn't appropriate for someone at his level in the firm, or the new level he'd be placed at shortly. George reached into the glove box for an envelope, one of four that contained keys to another block of flats they'd acquired and done up.

He knocked on Ichabod's door, feeling proper good for the first time in ages. The Brothers might be arseholes a lot of the time, but they also did nice things, and this was one of them. It was Mum's influence. She'd done good whenever she could, and George wanted to be more like her.

Could he rewrite his life? Begin again?

Ichabod appeared on the threshold. He'd smartened himself up recently, George's suggestion, and no longer resembled a lanky streak of piss but a man in a tidy suit with a decent haircut and shoes instead of trainers.

"Mornin', boss," he said. "Got a job for me?"

"Yep. Moving a load of stuff. I need to arrange for a van, though. I'll message Dwayne in a sec, he can go and pick one up."

"It'll be nicked van, then, if he's involved, so what dodgy business will I be doin'?"

"Nothing dodgy, and are you going to keep me out on your doorstep all fucking day or what?"

Ichabod stepped back. "Feck, where are me manners?" He led the way upstairs to his little home and gestured to the small breakfast bar with only one stool beneath it. "No room tae swing a cat in here."

"That's what today's job is. You're moving out. Moving up."

"Eh?"

George handed him the envelope. "Flat four, Regent Avenue. Rent's reduced because you work for us. Five hundred a month, docked out of your wages."

"Feckin' hell, that's...I don't know what tae say. I'm going up in the world then, eh?"

"We all are, mate. We've got an idea up our sleeve, and it's time to make a few changes around Cardigan, starting with that shitty casino at Entertainment Plaza."

"Give it a Whirl?"

George winced. "That name's being changed for a start."

"Feck, that's big news. Ye'll be grand, running that."

George smiled. "Nah, you will be."

"What?"

"You heard. Now get packing. There's a lot to discuss, so I'll give you two days to settle in, then we'll have a chat at Debbie's to go over the finer details."

Ichabod's smile was all the thanks George needed. He'd made a difference, had done something nice to counteract the icky feeling the Janet saga had inspired in him. Now, he could move on and throw himself into getting the casino refurbished and up and running.

He thought about the name he and Greg had finally agreed on.

Jackpot Palace, the idea pinched from a Vegas casino, was going to change everything.

Chapter Twenty-Three

Jackpot Palace hummed with the hustle and bustle of casino life, people throwing away their hard-earned money on a roll of the dice or a hunch on a roulette ball hitting the black or red. Karen Jacobs loved working here and had done so for six months. As well as being a croupier, she was the twins' eyes and ears. Or one of them anyway. Every employee in Jackpot had to keep on their toes, listen to conversations, and feed back any information to The Brothers. They'd had to pledge allegiance and all that bollocks.

She always marvelled at how it was just like being in Vegas the minute she walked through the front doors for a shift. The East End was left behind, and she immersed herself in the atmosphere, hobnobbing with the rich and famous as well as mere mortals.

The man on the blackjack table, Teddy Marshall, dealt the cards and made out he wasn't watching the players, when of course, he bloody was, along with the hidden cameras. Karen stood next to him, eye candy and a general distraction to the men seated around the table, or there to encourage them to go big or go home.

A wide bloke in his fifties won, and he drew the stack of chips towards him, a total of seven grand. Karen anticipated earning that much, and she would eventually, once the plans to rob the casino had been sorted. She and every other employee had been through the spiel with The Brothers prior to being taken on, them making it clear what would happen if anyone crossed them, but she wasn't worried about those two, not when she had Goldie in her corner, the brains behind the robbery.

She smiled at the players as Teddy dealt another round of cards, acting the part, keeping to her side of the bargain. Goldie had told her she had to prove her loyalty to George and Greg before the team swept in and stole the cash so they wouldn't suspect her.

Ichabod, the manager, prowled close by, hands held behind his back, his skinny frame appearing even more so in his classy suit. Expensive shoes covered his massive feet, and he had a presence about him now, one that hadn't been in evidence when the place had just opened. He'd clearly had lessons in how to conduct himself. The Irishman was a good sort, and she was a little sad to be duping him, but when it came to a big payday, any emotions towards him went out of the window.

She needed the money.

She glanced at Teddy who smiled and winked.

The pair of them were in on this, and they'd do whatever Goldie said. It wasn't just about the cash, their lives were on the line. If they fucked up, they'd be dead, and it wouldn't be the twins who killed them.

It would be Goldie, leader of The Golden Eye Estate.

To be continued in *Roulette,*
The Cardigan Estate 20

Printed in Great Britain
by Amazon